100 Lunches

A Gourmet Comedy

by
Jack Sharkey
and Leo W. Sears

A Samuel French Acting Edition

Samuel French
FOUNDED 1830

SAMUELFRENCH.COM

ISBN   978-0-573-69114-0   Printed   in   U.S.A.   #16988

MUSIC USE NOTE

Licensees are solely responsible for obtaining formal written permission from copyright owners to use copyrighted music in the performance of this play and are strongly cautioned to do so. If no such permission is obtained by the licensee, then the licensee must use only original music that the licensee owns and controls. Licensees are solely responsible and liable for all music clearances and shall indemnify the copyright owners of the play and their licensing agent, Samuel French, Inc., against any costs, expenses, losses and liabilities arising from the use of music by licensees.

IMPORTANT BILLING AND CREDIT REQUIREMENTS

All producers of *100 LUNCHES must* give credit to the Authors of the Play in all programs distributed in connection with performances of the Play, and in all instances in which the title of the Play appears for the purposes of advertising, publicizing or otherwise exploiting the Play and/or a production. The names of the Authors *must* appear on a separate line on which no other name appears, immediately following the title and *must* appear in size of type not less than fifty percent of the size of the title type.

100 LUNCHES

Cast of Characters

CHARLTON (CHUCK) REYNOLDS — successful writer of
stage mysteries, 35

CHARITY STARR — the only theatre critic who doesn't
like his worksmanship, 25–30

GLINDA BELLOWS — Chuck's housekeeper, named for
the Good Witch of the North, 50ish

TERRY REYNOLDS — Chuck's son, a smart (but not
smartaleck) matchmaker, 10–14

YOLANDA WEINTRAUB — sexy-but-predatory neighbor
lady, aggressively attractive, 30–40

WAITER — a multiple role of many "brothers" in a large
family of waiters, 25–?

BASIC SET: Livingroom of Reynolds home on Long
Island, N.Y., a comfortable and homey milieu, fur-
nished in expensive-but-not-gaudy good taste

MINI-SETS: A series of both classy and ghastly restaurants in Manhattan (this is actually just one set, but with
decor-changes suitable to whichever restaurant Chuck
and Charity are attending, with just space enough for
table, chairs and the itinerary of the Waiter — and some-
times Yolanda)

100 Lunches by Jack Sharkey and Leo W. Sears, directed by Peter J. Hill, with set design by Peter J. Hill, was premiered by Leo W. Sears at METRO PLAYHOUSE DINNER THEATRE at THE CLUB-Belaire, in Phoenix, Arizona on Wednesday night, January 11, 1989 with the following cast:

Chuck	Leo W. Sears
Charity	Sheree Spargo
Glinda	Delorez West
Terry	Jeff Sears
Yolanda	Laura Sadowski
Waiter(s)	Jack Dwyer

Act One

Setting: Living room of the Reynolds home on Long Island, N.Y. The morning after the opening night party following the New York premiere of Charlton Reynolds' latest stage mystery *How to Murder a Millionaire*.

Act Two

Lunch #1 — Chateau Jasper
  Home Interlude
Lunch #8 — Hymie's Hash House
  Home Interlude
Lunch #27 — The Four Seasons
  Home Interlude
Lunch #42 — Kali's Kosher Kitchen
  Home Interlude
Lunch #50 — Wally's Wiener World
  Home Interlude
Lunch #77 — Pierre's Palais de Pompe
  Home Interlude
Lunch #99 — Jose Wong's
  Home scene

Act Three

ABOUT THIS PLAY

Lest you imagine the central nub of our show is far-fetched: Back in the early 1960's, when BYE BYE BIR-DIE premiered on Broadway, the New York Times reviewer gave it a dreadful panning, ending the scathing review with the phrase ". . . neither fish nor fowl nor musical comedy." But every *other* newspaper in town gave the show total-rave notices. And about two days later, there showed up in the Times a review entitled "A SECOND LOOK AT *BYE BYE BIRDIE*" — and it, too, was an absolute rave. While we can only theorize about what went on at that reviewer's editorial offices in the interim, we suspect our own shows' plot-surprise is mighty close to the mark. Truth *is* a bit stranger than fiction.

"100 Lunches"

ACT ONE

The morning after opening-night party following NYC premiere of Chuck's latest stage mystery HOW TO MURDER A MILLIONAIRE. At curtain-rise, GLINDA Enters living room from kitchen. She pauses to survey pieces of tuxedo strewn about room. She then proceeds to pick up jacket, tie, pants, socks and shoes. One of shoes has liquid in it, which she pours into plant on desk top.

CHUCK. (*Off stage*) Did you check the porch roof?

GLINDA. (*with arms full of clothes*) At the risk of life and limb.

CHUCK. (O.S.) Of *all* days for the paper to be late—!

GLINDA. The world is full of newsstands, and you know how to drive. (*Places clothes over arm of sofa.*)

CHUCK. (O.S.) But I like to read the paper with my morning coffee!

GLINDA. I can always put a thermos in the car.

CHUCK. (O.S.) Why aren't you ever around when I *need* funny dialogue?! (*door-slam, off*)

GLINDA. (*belatedly*) Enjoy your shower! (*Starts for kitchen-exit, stops as TERRY, arms full of newspapers, Enters from front door.*) Aren't you a little *young* to be getting home at this hour?

TERRY. (*crosses to sofa and dumps papers on sofa*) I've been out stealing newspapers from the neighbors' driveways.

GLINDA. Going to be a lot of messy birdcages on our block.

TERRY. Did you *see* today's Manhattan Journal?

GLINDA. No, but if *you* did, tell your father before he boils over in the shower.

TERRY. I can't. It has the review of Pop's opening last night!

GLINDA. (*intuitively*) Charity Starr strikes again?

TERRY. With both fangs. She won't have any venom in her poison-sacs for a week!

GLINDA. That bad?

TERRY. (*after furtive look around*) See for yourself. (*Lifts sofa-cushion, produces own paper already folded open to theatre page.*) She's in *really* rare form.

GLINDA. (*takes paper, sits on arm of sofa, reads aloud slowly*) "*How to Murder a Millionaire*, the latest stage-play by perennial playwright Charlton Reynolds, is an amazingly successful mystery with almost countless victims . . ." (*pauses to observe*) Why, *that's* not bad at *all*!

TERRY. (*grimly*) Read on.

GLINDA. (*doing so*) "Unfortunately, the victims are the people who paid good money to attend the premiere" — Oh, dear! — "and the mystery is why this play was ever produced in the first place." Does — does it get any better, Terry?

TERRY. If you're a masochist, you'll adore every word.

GLINDA. (*with waning enthusiasm, reads a bit further*) "The problem with the play — for want of a better name — is that its central theme is murder — but how can one convincingly kill off characters who never were alive in the first place? Reynolds' lack of skill in creating recognizable human beings to people the stage makes murder almost redundant. If his unaccountable popularity with audiences is a case of the blind leading the blind, perhaps it's because his murder mysteries are a case of the dead killing the dead." (*hands newspaper to TERRY*) You shouldn't have stolen the neighbors' newspapers. You should have blown up the newspaper office.

TERRY. I didn't have trainfare to Manhattan. (*Starts to pick up papers.*)

GLINDA. I would've lent you my car.

TERRY. But where would I get a bomb?

GLINDA. (*indicates newspaper she holds*) You could have used your father's play. (*reacts*) I hear him coming! Quick, hide this! No—(*grabs it back*)—give it to me! Stall him in here for a minute! (*Exits to kitchen.*)

(*TERRY quickly hides papers: in desk drawer, under chair, in plant, under couch cushion, etc., then leans nonchalantly against wall; an instant later, CHUCK Enters from sleeping-area.*)

TERRY. (*all innocence*) Hi, Pop! Why don't you sit down and I'll bring your breakfast on a tray?

CHUCK. Terry, I'll admit I was partying to all hours, but I can still make it to the kitchen.

TERRY. But it's a sunny morning and the kitchen faces east.

CHUCK. (*Winces via eye-crinkling*) How sunny?

TERRY. How heavy were you partying? (*Waves sock at him from clothing pile*)

CHUCK. (*hesitates, then sits in armchair*) Only until the first reviews came out. They were nice. We should have a good run. But I gave up waiting for the *Manhattan Journal.* Must be a real doozy of a review for Queen Cobra to take so long writing it.

TERRY. (*inadvertently*) You can say *that* again!

CHUCK. What—?

TERRY. I mean—when she took so long—it—uh—*must* be a doozy.

CHUCK. (*stands*) You've seen it!

TERRY. (*valliantly*) Seen what?

CHUCK. Now, look, son—(*pauses as GLINDA re-*

enters with neatly folded newspaper!)

GLINDA. *Here* you are, Mr. Reynolds! I'll just go get your coffee! (*turns and starts for kitchen*)

CHUCK. (*unfolding paper*) Is Charity Starr's review in here, Glinda?

GLINDA. (*pauses short of Exit*) I'm sure I don't know, sir. I only glanced through it looking for shopping coupons. (*at this point, he opens paper and we see large cut-out area; when he reacts, she continues*) I found some. (*from behind CHUCK, TERRY gives her a thumb-and-forefinger-circle "okay" sign of approval*)

CHUCK. But where's the *theatre*-review section?

TERRY. Must've been on the back of those coupons.

GLINDA. Right!

CHUCK. So bring me the *coupons*, then!

GLINDA. Can't. I already used them.

CHUCK. Mrs. Bellows, *where* can you go shopping on Long Island for groceries at seven-thirty in the morning?!

GLINDA. Uh — *Seven-Eleven*?

CHUCK. What were we *out* of — *Slurpees*?

TERRY. They're awfully hard to keep refrigerated . . .

CHUCK. (*looks from one to the other; then, quietly*) Let's see the review.

GLINDA. How about some nice breakfast first!

CHUCK. I don't *feel* like a Slurpee right now. (*GLINDA winces, sighs, Exits to kitchen.*)

TERRY. Don't be too sure — they're great for cooling you off . . .

CHUCK. That bad?

TERRY. (*as GLINDA re-enters with neatly-cut-out review*) See for yourself.

CHUCK. (*takes review, looks from one to the other, moves to sofa & sits, then starts reading, to himself, mumbling a word here and there, and getting angrier with each mumble:)* "never alive in the first place"! . . . ". . . unaccountable popularity . . ."! . . . ". . . *blind leading the blind*"! . . . "*dead killing the dead*" —?! *(abruptly crumbles review between his hands with a motion not unlike throttling)* Why that — no-good — vicious — heartless — insensitive —*(rises)*

GLINDA. Terry, if you won't leave the room, you'd better cover your ears.

CHUCK. This is a disaster! What am I going to do?! *(sits again)*

GLINDA. Well, you can always get a job at Long Island University *teaching* playwriting!

CHUCK. Are you crazy? I *can't* teach playwriting! I don't know how it's *done*!

TERRY. *(moves to sit on sofa arm)* Then how do you keep *doing* it, Dad?

CHUCK. It's like riding a bicycle — once you *learn*, you just keep *on* doing it. But I haven't the *vaguest* idea how to *teach* somebody to ride!

TERRY. So *that's* why I keep falling off!

GLINDA. But Mister Reynolds, there must be *something* you could tell a class . . . ?

CHUCK. Oh, sure: Dream up a plot, name your characters, give them something to say, and when they've said enough, drop the curtain!

GLINDA. You made it sound so *easy*!

CHUCK. It *is* easy. For *me*. But imagine how frustrated those *pupils* would get. You just heard my *entire* lecture for the whole semester!

GLINDA. Amazing! All that talent — and no way to *share* any of it!

TERRY. The *other* reviews were *great*, Dad.

CHUCK. Charity Starr has soured me on *all* critics!
She's ruined my morning, upset my stomach, and probably destroyed my career!

GLINDA. Can't you *do* something about her?

CHUCK. Short of manually *strangling* her, (*rises*) I
don't know what. (*Crumbles newspaper with a definite
strangling — motion, drops it to floor.*) I'm going for a
walk. (*goes as far as front door, turns to add*) I'll either
come back calm and refreshed — or a wanted murderer!
(*Starts to Exit.*)

(*Before he can Exit, YOLANDA WEINTRAUB Enters
via front door; 30–40 years old, quite attractive vi-
sually, but on the aggressive side in personality,
makeup and dress.*)

YOLANDA. Poor Chucky! Have you recovered from
that nasty woman's vile review?

(*Though CHUCK obviously appreciates this balm on his
wounds, we can see that GLINDA and TERRY are
not exactly crazy about this newcomer, though they
politely conceal it. TERRY moves to chair & sits.*)

CHUCK. Nice of you to be concerned, Yolanda. Yeah,
I guess I'm okay. but I'd better not *see* her for at least
twenty-four hours!

YOLANDA. I came over as soon as read that vicious
attack. (*Drags him to and plumps him down onto sofa,
starts massaging his neck from behind, which he obviously loves.*) I thought you might need someone to help
you recover.

GLINDA. That *walk* would do you a *lot* more good, sir.

TERRY. Yeah, Dad, if you get *too* relaxed you can't
create worth a darn.

YOLANDA. (*massaging away*) But you *should* learn to relax, Chucky! You work *much* too hard, and how you get any sleep with the late *hours* you keep—!

CHUCK. Can't help it. I write when inspiration strikes, and it tends to strike hardest about three o'clock in the morning!

YOLANDA. Is your bedroom soundproofed—?

TERRY. Why?

GLINDA. What do you have in mind?

YOLANDA. (*stops massaging, flustered*) I just meant that if Chucky finally decides to *remarry*, his early-morning typing might be a *disturbance* to his new bride —unless the room has soundproofing so she won't hear his typewriter, see?

GLINDA. (*with extra meaning*) I certainly *do* see!

TERRY. (*aside to GLINDA:*) I wish I *didn't*!

CHUCK. (*Attempts to stand but YOLANDA pushes back down.*) I've really got to take that walk. (*Tries again but YOLANDA pushes him down again.*) I'm too uptight to get *anything* done 'til I blow off some steam!

YOLANDA. Would you like *me* to walk along *with* you, Chucky?

GLINDA. You'd need track shoes!

TERRY. Dad moves *much* too fast for you to keep up!

CHUCK. (*escapes her grasp & stands*) They're right, Yolanda. (*Crosses around sofa to YOLANDA.*) Besides, I plan to do a lot of cussing under my breath, and you might get an education in vocabulary you'd rather avoid! Excuse me! (*Exits*)

YOLANDA. That poor dear tormented man! (*starts for front door, murmuring half to herself*) I'm *sure* I have a pair of track shoes *someplace* in the house . . . (*Exits*)

GLINDA. Your father doesn't need a housekeeper, he needs a *bouncer*! There goes an unhappy camper.

TERRY. Dad or Miss Weintraub?

GLINDA. Oh, *she's* happy enough. A praying mantis *enjoys* massaging the neck of its prey before devouring it! I meant your father. This newspaper review has hit him harder than usual.

TERRY. What was your first clue? Dad seems to be getting more and more upset with each review by that Charity Starr.

GLINDA. Maybe she's finally pushed him over the edge. He could decide to give up writing and take up acting. (*pause; GLINDA & TERRY react with distaste*) Is anyone holding auditions for *THE BOSTON STRANGLER*?

TERRY. (*moving toward the front door; picks up books from desk*) No, but dad's got a great candidate for the lead in the remake of *THE TOWERING INFERNO*. On top of that bonfire, her review could hardly say, "It wasn't so hot!"

GLINDA. Where are you going?

TERRY. (*stopping at front door*) It's a school day. Thought I might drop in on my class.

GLINDA. *Not* before you return *every one* of those stolen newspapers to the neighbors, young man!

TERRY. (*Puts down book and collects newspapers.*) Aw, with the state of World News today, I'm doing them a favor.

GLINDA. There's more than news in the paper. You know Mrs. Pomeroy—Nellie has to read today's horoscope before she'll go out of the house.

TERRY. Oh—okay. (*starts for door again*) I *wish* there were some way to get that Starr woman to see the light, though.

GLINDA. We could put her in *THE PHANTOM OF THE OPERA* and drop a chandelier on her.

TERRY. (*pauses at the door*) Even better—put her in *THE UNSKINKABLE MOLLY BROWN*!

GLINDA. As Molly?

TERRY. No. The iceberg.

GLINDA. Oh, get out of here and return those newspapers!

TERRY. Okay, okay, I'm going.

(*As TERRY Exits through front door, we hear BACK DOOR CLOSE off in kitchen, and even as GLINDA looks that way, CHUCK Enters, striding toward bedroom.*)

CHUCK. I just remembered: I *hate* taking long walks! (*starts out to bedroom*) Is there any poison in the medicine cabinet?

GLINDA. Classic or sugar-free?

CHUCK. (*pauses*) I'm in no mood to make decisions. (*Exits-reenters*) I can always use my razor—except I hate pain. (*Exits-reenters*) You know what I don't understand? *What* does that gal have *against* me? It's like trying to entertain a black widow spider! (*Exits-reenters*) It's not the bad reviews—I get them from *other* critics occasionally—it's the *consistent* bad reviews. (*Exits-reenters*) There must be something I've done, that I don't know about, to keep her in a constant state of revenge!

GLINDA. To get her *that* venomous, you'd have to have wiped out several generations of her family.

CHUCK. (*crosses to sofa and sits*) Unless she just *enjoys* injecting her poison?

GLINDA. I know what you mean. The *best* review she ever gave you was announcing she was taking her *vacation* rather than attend the opening of your mystery BLOOD ON HER HANDS. (*Exits to kitchen.*)

CHUCK. Yeah, but she sank her fangs in as soon as she got back. And I *quote*: "This play should have been called BLOOD ON *HIS* HANDS, because Mister Reynolds is single-handedly killing off the murder-mystery genre with his mechanical plots and cardboard characters"! (*thoughtfully*) I wonder—do you know if a murderer can *really* get a jury of his *actual* peers?? With twelve *playwrights* on the panel, I could murder her in Times Square and still get off with a Not Guilty.

GLINDA. (*Reenters*) I wouldn't count on it. You may be a fellow-playwright, but you are also their *competition*!

CHUCK. (*stands*) Damn. Never thought of that. Hell, I'm going back to bed.

(*CHUCK Exits to bedroom and then TERRY re-enters at front door.*)

TERRY. Two of the neighbors caught me returning the paper. I had to say I was the new delivery boy!

GLINDA. Bad move. Now when they read that review, they're going to think you *had* to take the job since your father can no longer support the family!

TERRY. That darn Charity Starr! How can somebody who looks so great have such a vengeful heart?

GLINDA. How do you know she looks so great?

TERRY. Remember? I pointed her out to you last night. She was the one in the black dress. (*moves to sofa & sits*)

GLINDA. That's right. Black. What else would a black widow wear? I wonder if she has an orange hour-glass on her belly? So you thought she was attractive?

TERRY. Yeah, (*longingly*) she was dynamite. (*Back to reality*) That is . . . for a poisonous spider.

GLINDA. Hmmm.

TERRY. She sure is getting to Dad. He works so hard all the time. It's not fair.

GLINDA. Terry, it comes with the territory. It's like ants at a picnic. You try to enjoy yourself in spite of them. (*picks up clothes & takes them to kitchen*)

TERRY. But, it's getting to the point where he's not enjoying himself. I mean he never goes out; all he does is write. And it's been that way since Mom died two years ago. (*pause*) Glinda, I sure miss her. I know Dad does too.

GLINDA. (*Reenters and sits on sofa next to TERRY*) We all do.

TERRY. I think that's why he pushes himself so much. He doesn't deserve the aggravation.

GLINDA. Part of being a playwright is having to suffer the slings and arrows of the critics.

TERRY. But, he works so hard; he's successful. The audiences like his plays. The actors like his plays. And most critics like his plays . . . everyone except our resident grinch.

GLINDA. As long as the audiences and actors love his stuff what difference does it make what Ms. Charity Starr thinks?

TERRY. Other than ruining his mood, I guess it makes absolutely *no* difference.

GLINDA. Right! So, lighten up! (*stands and moves behind sofa*) You're starting to take this whole thing too seriously. It's more fun to conjure up images of how to get even.

TERRY. Yeah, like we could lure her into a room and force her to sit through fifty-three straight hours of *THE BRADY BUNCH* and *THE PARTRIDGE FAMILY.*

GLINDA. Not bad. Sort of sugar her to death. How about . . . we could glue popcorn all over her and drop her off at Central Park to feed the pigeons.

TERRY. Very creative. How about we kidnap her, give

her a Brian Bosworth haircut, a BORN TO KILL tattoo and drop her off at a Hell's Angels bar?

GLINDA. Too cruel. (*looks at watch*) I hate to stop all the fun, but don't you have to get to school?

TERRY. But, I was just getting started.

GLINDA. No buts. (*Points to door.*) School, buster. Besides I've got work to do.

TERRY. (*stands*) But, Dad's going to need my support!

GLINDA. (*Moves to TERRY and gently maneuvers him toward front door.*) Fine. You go to school. Learn. Graduate. Go to college. Become a lawyer. Get rich and support him in his old age.

TERRY. But I mean this morning.

GLINDA. I'll take care of him. You're going to miss your bus.

TERRY. (*Pauses at front door.*) That's okay. Didn't you read the report that just came out that said that busing has done nothing to improve education?

GLINDA. You are stalling. If you miss your bus and your Dad has to drive you, he is going to be even more upset. So . . . hit the door (*She opens the door*)

TERRY. Fine. I'm gone. I'm outa here. I'm . . .

GLINDA. Bye! (*She shoves him out, and closes the door. She starts to step away from the door. DOOR BELL rings repeatedly. She opens door.*)

TERRY. (*rushing in*) I think I could learn a lot more if I took my books. (*he picks up books from desk and runs back out. GLINDA starts to close the door. TERRY sticks head back in*) Isn't education a wonderful thing? Bye!

GLINDA. (*closes door*) That kid! (*GLINDA starts toward kitchen, but is interrupted by CHUCK's entry*) I thought you went back to bed.

CHUCK. I can't sleep when I'm hungry. And I completely missed my breakfast.

GLINDA. (*starts for kitchen*) I'll get right on it!

CHUCK. Won't that make it hard to eat?

GLINDA. Okay, I'll get *to* it! Better?

CHUCK. Much. (*sits as she starts to Exit again*) Did Terry get off to school okay?

GLINDA. Well, he left in time to catch the bus. My responsibility ends at the front door.

CHUCK. (*reading*) Oh, hell! (*Crosses to GLINDA and points to front page.*) He's *got* no school today!

GLINDA. (*Looks at paper.*) *Another* teachers' strike? This is becoming an annual event!

CHUCK. He's got a long bus ride for nothing, poor kid.

GLINDA. Unless the bus company *knows* about the strike—? (*starts for front door*) I'd better see if I can catch him.

CHUCK. (*Exits to kitchen*) If you can't, I'll drive over to the school and pick him up.

(*DOOR BELL*)

GLINDA. (*opens door*) Yes?

CHARITY. Hello. I'm Charity Starr. (*GLINDA slams door. DOOR BELL again. GLINDA reopens door reluctantly. CHARITY steps inside; she has a rolled-up and ribbon-bow-bound newspaper in one hand.*) I need to speak to Mr. Reynolds.

GLINDA. Are you sure it's safe?

CHARITY. I'm willing to chance it. Am I too early?

GLINDA. For what?

CHARITY. Well, I thought playwrights kept late hours at the theatre and usually slept in, mornings. I can come back later, if you like.

GLINDA. Mister Reynolds was up with the robins. He didn't want to miss your review.

CHARITY. Oh, dear. That must have really gotten his day off to a soggy start.

GLINDA. Why don't you ask him yourself? Have a seat while I get him.

CHARITY. Thank you. (*sits, looks around room*) You certainly have a lovely place here.

GLINDA. Enjoy it while it lasts. After Mister Reynolds finds you here, the place may be reduced to rubble! (*starts for kitchen*) I hope you know how to dodge.

CHARITY. (*stands up*) Maybe—I *should* come back later on. Or phone for an appointment. Or—

CHUCK. (*off*) Glinda, who was at the door?

GLINDA. Charity Starr!

CHUCK. (*sound of breaking glass than a bull roar*) Aaaagh?!

CHARITY. (*heading for front door*) You know, I think I *will* make an appointment first—!

(*Before CHARITY can reach the doorknob, door flies open and an ecstatic TERRY rushes in with his schoolbooks, blocking her retreat as he happily slams door.*)

TERRY. There's a teachers' strike!

GLINDA. Miss Starr, may I introduce the Town Crier?

TERRY. *Charity* Starr?! . . . Oh, sure, *now* I recognize you! You looked different in that slinky black dress last night.

CHARITY. You mean the *opening*?

CHUCK. (*Enters from kitchen wielding steak knife and bandaged finger*) *Where* is she?!

CHARITY. (*gets behind TERRY, using him like a shield*) Mister Reynolds, *control* yourself!

CHUCK. First you ravage my play, now you're trying to strangle my son!

TERRY. (*getting out of her frantic grasp*) *Dad*—aren't you being a bit *drastic*—?

CHUCK. (*looks at knife, reacts, hands it to GLINDA*) I couldn't tear the adhesive tape tape with my teeth. (*holds up gauzed-and-taped finger*) Those coffee cup splinters are *sharp*!

CHARITY. Then you *weren't* trying to *stab* me?

CHUCK. (*icily*) That would be *much* too quick!

GLINDA. (*taking knife, heads kitchenward*) I'll just tidy up the debris. (*Exits*)

TERRY. Dad, what's *Miss Starr* doing here? (*to CHARITY*) You got a *death wish* or something?

CHARITY. Well, I *did* want to *discuss* something with your father—uh—?

TERRY. Terry.

CHARITY. Terry. But if this is a bad time—?

CHUCK. (*Points at sofa*) Sit there! (*she sits instantly*) Terry, go someplace.

TERRY. (*gleefully*) No witnesses, right?

CHARITY. Listen, I can see you're very busy, so why don't I—(*starts to leave*)

CHUCK. *Sit*! (*she sits and puts newspaper that she was carrying on table; then to TERRY:*) *Go*! (*To GLINDA*) *Coffee*! (*GLINDA and TERRY Exit to kitchen*)

TERRY. (O.S.) Can I at least listen to her screams—?

CHARITY. He's kidding, isn't he?

CHUCK. We'll *see*. (*moves to sofa near her, sits facing her, his manner wary*) Now, exactly *what* possible reason could you have to expose yourself to mortal peril this way?

CHARITY. I gather you didn't like my review of your play. (*holds up newspaper*)

CHUCK. Did you *expect* me to?

CHARITY. Well, everyone can use a little constructive

criticism, now and then, so if you approached my review with an open mind—

CHUCK. (*calls off*) Terry, get ready to listen to her screams.

CHARITY. (*Stands*) *Let me re-phrase that*!

TERRY. (*off*) Aw, you can scream better than *that*!

CHARITY. (*screams off*) *I WAS NOT SCREAMING!*

TERRY. (*Reenters*) There, that's *much* better!

GLINDA. (*Comes after TERRY*) Terry, mind your manners. Miss Starr is a *guest*!

TERRY. You mean like a guest at a necktie party? (*Mimics hanging*)

CHUCK. (*Stands. To CHARITY*) Sit! (*She sits*) (*To TERRY*) Go! (*To GLINDA*) Coffee! (*GLINDA & TERRY Exit. CHUCK sits.*) Now, do you feel better, getting that out of your system?

CHARITY. No. I do not. You ought to be *ashamed*, making me lose control.

CHUCK. I ought to be ashamed?

TERRY. (*peeking in*) You're lucky you're not being ripped to shreds.

CHUCK. Terry!

CHARITY. I thought my coming over here was a good idea. I thought it would give us a chance to clear the air. But, I can leave if . . .

CHUCK. Since you've already entered the cave of the bear . . .

GLINDA. (*peeking in*) I tried to warn you.

CHUCK. Obviously, very good advice. (*to GLINDA*) Don't you have some breakfast to fix, Mrs. Bellows? (*GLINDA backs out*)

CHARITY. (*stands*) Oh . . . I didn't mean to disturb your breakfast.

CHUCK. (*stands so that he and CHARITY are nose to*

nose) Why should this morning be any different? You've disturbed my breakfast after every opening night review you've ever written. This time you just decided to do it in person.

CHARITY. Well?

CHUCK. Well, what?

CHARITY. Do we clear the air or not?

CHUCK. It's up to you.

CHARITY. Can we act civilized?

CHUCK. *I* am always civilized.

CHARITY. Fine. (*sits*)

CHUCK. Fine. (*sits*)

CHARITY. Now that we're all comfy and cozy—

CHUCK. Speak for yourself.

CHARITY. —I'd like to ask you a favor.

CHUCK. (*calls kitchenward*) Glinda, get the Guinness people on the phone—I think we've just had the new world's record for all-out high-faluting *gall*!

GLINDA. (*leans head in*) What was the *old* world's record?

TERRY. (*vaudeville entrance from kitchen*) When the executioner asked Joan of Arc if he could borrow a *match*!

CHARITY. (*stands*) Look, I *thought* we were going to be *civilized*, but if you—

CHUCK. (*to CHARITY:*) Sit! (*CHARITY sits; CHUCK stares at GLINDA & TERRY*)

TERRY. Go! (*Exits*)

GLINDA. Coffee! (*Exits*)

CHUCK. (*Sits. With icy politeness*) You were saying—?

CHARITY. I'm writing a play, and I need your help with it.

CHUCK. (*bounds to his feet and crosses to chair*) *That*

even beats Joan of Arc! This morning you ripped my new play to shreds with your poison pen, and now you expect *me* to help you run the *shredder*?!

CHARITY. I suppose it *does* sound a bit *audacious* of me —

CHUCK. (*plops into chair again, shaking his head in stunned wonderment*) "*Audacious*"?! I think "*deranged*" is closer to the mark! After you go and tell the entire civilized world — the members who can *read*, anyhow — that as a playwright I make a good *cardboard*-manufacturer, you're suddenly here to hitch a free ride on my *expertise* in the field?!

CHARITY. (*Crosses to chair*) I *never* said you were an incompetent. I just said your *characters* stunk!

CHUCK. (*Stands. Facetiously*) Oh, and here I was acting cross as a bear! What ever possessed me!

(*CHUCK backs CHARITY across stage, up onto and across coffee table to front of sofa during the following*)

CHARITY. Mister Reynolds, be fair. I never said you were a bad *play*-writer; I *like* your plays. And I especially marvel at your ability to construct *plots*, mechanical or not. The only thing I don't enjoy is the two-dimensional nature of your characters. The story-lines have always been nothing but brilliant.

CHUCK. (*confused*) Then why didn't you say as much to your *readers*?

CHARITY. I *did*, if you'd take the time to read my review in its *entirety*. (*sits on sofa*)

GLINDA. (*leans out of kitchen*) You know, she *did* say the *mystery*-part was perfectly swell, sir. Of course, that came about three paragraphs after your *characters* went into the *threshing*-machine.

TERRY. (*also leans out*) And she's got *great* legs!

CHUCK. (*stands*) Terry—!

TERRY. I'm going, I'm going! (*Exits into kitchen*)

GLINDA. I'm coffeeing, I'm coffeeing! (*Exits into kitchen*)

(*CHUCK stares at CHARITY.*)

CHARITY. (*comes to her feet*) Look, we'll never get *anywhere* with "Mr. and Mrs. Interlocutor" at the ready in the next room. Isn't there somewhere *else* we could have this discussion?

CHUCK. How about the prize ring in Madison Square Garden? We could sell tickets.

CHARITY. Seriously.

CHUCK. (*Crosses around back of sofa to CHARITY'S right shoulder.*) I must admit—I'm fascinated by your sheer *nerve*, Miss Starr. And—I also must admit—it's kind of a *nice* feeling to, as it were, have you "at my mercy" in this matter . . .

CHARITY. Which you do. My own playwriting is totally dependent upon your answer.

CHUCK. Let me get this straight—you've written a play, and—

CHARITY. (*stands*) Not quite. I'm *trying* to write a play, a play with well-rounded, believable characters, but my *story*-line just won't jell. I scribble out all sorts of scenes with marvelous depth and meaning and purpose —and they just *sit* there, with nowhere to go. (*crosses* C.) So—I thought I'd ask the help of an *expert*. When it comes to *plots*, no one in theatre can touch you!

CHUCK. (*Crosses* R. *around sofa and sits*) Damn, How can I maintain my loathing of you if you keep ladling *honey* all over me?

TERRY. (*off*) Careful she doesn't stake you to an *ant-hill*!

GLINDA. (*off*) Terry, *shush*!

CHARITY. (*Crosses to sofa and sits.*) See what I mean?

CHUCK. It *is* kind of like sharing a phonebooth with a built-in Greek Chorus. But—where *could* we meet? *My* office is out, what with Glinda and Terry likely to have their ears glued to the door—

GLINDA/TERRY. (*stage whispers-ad lib*) I told you we were too loud-Be quiet, etc.

CHARITY. And *my* office consists of a desk in the middle of twenty-three *identical* desks, all occupied by reporters typing or shouting on the telephone—

CHUCK. There's always the New York Public Library —except they'd keep *shushing* us.

CHARITY. There must be *some* place two people can converse in leisurely fashion without a lot of eavesdroppers or interruptions—

CHUCK. (*smacks one fist into palm of other hand*) A *restaurant*! It's perfect! We can go in, place our order—

CHARITY. (*similarly elated*)—and then have *hours* of time to talk before the order arrives!

CHARITY. I see *you* get the same kind of service *I* usually do!

CHARITY. You know, it'd be kind of *fun* doing it that way. There must be *thousands* of restaurants in Manhattan. We could "eat ethnic" and broaden our education at the same time!

CHUCK. How's that again?

CHARITY. You know, go Japanese one day, Armenian the next day, East Indian the third day—

CHUCK. You're starting to *get* to me. *I* love experimenting with new food-delights . . .

CHARITY. (*stands*) Then it's a deal—?

CHUCK. (*stands*) Under one condition.

CHARITY. What?

CHUCK. Since I'll be supplying some very expensive tutelage — you pick up all the checks!

CHARITY. You've got a deal! (*they handshake, briefly*) But before we do anything else, may I use your powder room? It's been a long drive out here . . .

CHUCK. (*pointing in whatever is the proper direction*) Oh, sure, it's right in there.

CHARITY. Thank you! (*Exits. CHUCK watches as CHARITY Exits and when she is off he does a celebration-revenge dance. This brings GLINDA and TERRY out of the kitchen. TERRY crosses to hallway to bedroom and stands guard.*)

GLINDA. Mister Reynolds, have you gone totally *bananas*? How can you *possibly* teach her playwriting? Not fifteen minutes ago, you were wailing that you don't have the vaguest idea *how* to teach it!

CHUCK. *She* won't know that! She couldn't learn anything even if I *could* teach! Did you *see* that neanderthal *brow* of hers?

TERRY. (*slightly defensive — after all, she is a knock-out*) *I* think it's a very *pretty* brow.

CHUCK. (*crosses to TERRY*) (*pointedly*) Maybe to another *neanderthal* . . . ! (*TERRY reacts*)

GLINDA. But — if I'm not being snoopy — or even if I *am* — just what *do* you intend to do at all those *lunches*?

CHUCK. (*Crosses to desk chair & sits.*) I intend to buy the most expensive meals I've ever eaten in my life! And I'll feed her a line of gibberish that'll just plain *destroy* any play she *is* working on! (*rubs his hands together with fiendish glee*) No matter *what* she's written, I'll tell her it's *all wrong*!

TERRY. (*crosses to Dad*) (*admiringly*) Why, Dad! You

do have the heart of a *fiend*! And here I was thinking you were such an *average* kind of guy! (*TERRY & CHUCK execute "high five" hand slap. TERRY resumes guarding.*)

GLINDA. I don't like it. Getting so worked up with your plotting, you'll *curdle* anything you eat! She'll get a rotten play, and you'll get terminal heartburn!

TERRY. Jiggers, here she comes back!

(*CHARITY re-enters. The three stare at CHARITY. She checks to see if something is amiss in her clothing. Pause. Then:*)

CHUCK. Well, when shall we begin? I can't do it today, unfortunately. I'm right in the middle of a new mystery and have to figure out who-done-it before I stage the murder. But — (*gets book out of desk drawer*) there *is* something you can read in the meantime. (*Stands and crosses to CHARITY*) Are you familiar with Georges Polti? (*hands her the book*) His book on plotting is a *must* for neophyte writers . . . (*crosses toward bedroom Exit*)

CHARITY. (*turns toward CHUCK*) You mean this is sort of my *homework* assignment, and tomorrow we'll have a short *quiz*?

CHUCK. (*with devious smile*) Something like that! (*Exits*)

GLINDA. I must say, Miss Starr, this thing has worked out better than I imagined. It's so nice to know you have a heart!

TERRY. Don't forget those *legs*! (*BOTH give him a look; he subsides.*)

GLINDA. I had no *idea* you were an aspiring playwright!

TERRY. Though Dad always says he suspects *all* reviewers are would-be playwrights.

GLINDA. Now, Terry, —

TERRY. He thinks they take out their failure as playwrights on the people who *can* write plays.

GLINDA. Terry—!

CHARITY. Well, he's wrong. And so are you, Mrs. Bellows.

GLINDA. I don't follow you—?

CHARITY. (*after a glance to be certain CHUCK isn't within earshot*) I've never written a play in my life! Or even *wanted* to.

TERRY. Then how come—?

CHARITY. (*draws them* D.S. *a bit, says in confidential tones:*) When I saw how *down* Mister Reynolds was, I realized I might be depriving the world of some *excellent* stage mysteries—cardboard characters or not—I knew I had to do *something* to relieve the unfair *burden* I'd placed on him. The theatre *needs* him too much.

GLINDA. But if you're *not* really writing a play—

TERRY. —and you *don't* have all those in-depth characters to trot out for Dad—

GLINDA/TERRY. —what are you going to do at all those *lunches*?

CHARITY. (*after a pause, to TERRY:*) I plan to *eat* (*to GLINDA:*) a lot!

CURTAIN

–End of Act One–

ACT II

LUNCH #1 CHATEAU JASPER

SETTING: As the scene opens CHUCK and CHARITY are seated at a restaurant table. WAITER approaches and realizes that they're glaring at each other. They do not respond to his arrival with their menus, so he uses the menus to break their stare-down.

CHARITY. I hear that this restaurant is one of the most expensive in New York!

CHUCK. Obviously my time is valuable. Think of all the time you're taking me away from my writing. I have plays that I'm working on: plays that put food on my table. I'm sure you'll find that I'm worth every cent you're spending on lunch. Besides, your paper's paying, isn't it?

CHARITY. I guess so I haven't figured out exactly how yet. (*opens menu*) I certainly can't afford this place. Everything is so overpriced.

WAITER. (*very snooty*) There's a MacDonald's down the street. Perhaps it would be more to your liking. They've got a special meal. You can get a cheeseburger, fries and a medium soft drink and you get a cute little plastic toy free. And just think, it comes in a cute little container that has these neat little puzzles all over it.

CHUCK. Are you trying to be funny?

WAITER. Why? Are you missing Ronald MacDonald?

CHUCK. Listen, we're here for a business luncheon. If I want insults I'll read one of Miss Starr's reviews.

WAITER. So, you're Charity Starr?

CHARITY. May we just order? (*closes menu.*)

WAITER. While you two kids are deciding, can I bring

you something from the bar? . . . We make a nifty Shirley Temple, and I can bring you two straws.

CHUCK. Bring us a bottle of champagne. Do you have Dom Perignon?

WAITER. (*attitude changes*) Yes, sir!

CHARITY. Just two iced teas, please.

CHUCK. Bring us the champagne.

CHARITY. Ice tea will do.

CHUCK. Champagne, please.

CHARITY. Who's paying for this?

CHUCK. Your paper, I believe. (*to WAITER:*) CHAMPAGNE!

CHARITY. We are *not* having a party. It's the middle of the day. Let's concentrate on business. (*to WAITER:*) Two iced teas, please.

WAITER. Have you two considered auditioning for a Miller Lite commercial? When you make up your mind, please let me know. We've got plenty of time. I get off in three hours.

CHUCK. Iced tea. (*to CHARITY:*) *THIS* time.

WAITER. Oh, joy! (*WAITER Exits.*)

CHARITY. Are you ready to discuss the ground rules?

CHUCK. Why don't we decide what we're going to eat? (*opens menu*) I'm starving.

CHARITY. What's more important? . . . Eating or teaching play writing?

CHUCK. I didn't have any breakfast, and I can't eat with my stomach growling.

CHARITY. Fine. (*Looks at menu.*)

CHUCK. Everything looks so good. (*WAITER Enters with iced tea.*) I'm going to have a hard time making up my mind.

WAITER. Oh, great!

CHUCK. (*not really hearing*) What?

WAITER. Oh, I'm in no real hurry . . . , my other customers always like a long wait before they order. It helps them build up an appetite. They'll appreciate the food that much more.

CHARITY. I'll just have the house salad with the house dressing.

CHUCK. I'll start with the jumbo shrimp cocktail. Then I'll have the spinach salad with hot mustard dressing. Then I'll be ready for the butterfly pork chops with the rice pilaf.

CHARITY. Are you sure that's all?

CHUCK. That's all. I'm eating light today.

WAITER. That meal could feed a light *infantry!* (*WAITER Exits.*)

CHARITY. Why do these expensive restaurants always have the rude waiters?

CHUCK. It's just part of their charm, I guess.

WAITER. (O.S.) Witch! (*This comment should not be heard by Chuck or Charity.*)

CHARITY. I wonder if our food critic has reviewed this place.

CHUCK. If he did and that critique did for this place what your review did for me, we'd better sit at different tables. We could pass notes . . . just in case they put a bomb in your salad.

CHARITY. Why? I didn't see a Reynolds' murder mystery on the menu.

CHARITY. (*Tone changes from playful to serious.*) Do you want to discuss the service or do you want to discuss the ground rules?

CHARITY. I thought you couldn't think until you'd eaten.

CHUCK. I'll struggle through.

CHARITY. Very well . . . it's really quite simple. I

buy you a lunch or two and you give me lessons on playwriting.

CHUCK. Hold on a minute! It's not so simple. Teaching something like this is like teaching sculpture. You don't have a quick lesson or two, then "Here's a pile of clay. Now Sculpt!" It takes a slow deliberate approach. We're going to do this right and take our time. You can't rush something like this.

CHARITY. So what did you have in mind?

CHUCK. Two things: First of all, we take very small pieces so that they are absorbed slowly. Secondly, as we go along, you will write a play and, if it's good enough, (*chuckles*) we'll try to get it produced.

CHARITY. That could take a lot of time. That's a lot of lunches.

CHUCK. If you want to back out now, that's up to you.

CHARITY. But that could be as many as a *hundred* lunches!

CHUCK. But where are you going to get such personalized service?

CHARITY. How am I going to explain that many lunches on my expense account? The paper's accountant is like a bulldog. I thought a couple of lunches wouldn't be a problem. But that many?

CHUCK. There's always one of those writers' correspondence schools. I stopped by a newstand on my way over and picked up one of their ads for you. (*Brings out comic book from inside jacket and shows her the writer's ad on the back.*)

CHARITY. No . . . I want to do it this way. Shall we start now?

(*WAITER Enters with shrimp cocktail and serves it to CHUCK.*)

CHUCK. Sorry. Not while I'm eating. (*Offers CHAR-ITY a shrimp.*) Are you sure you wouldn't like one of these? They're very good.

(*BLACKOUT. Change to living room scene while set is being changed for next lunch scene.*)

(*Living room, daytime. GLINDA's dusting. TERRY Enters from kitchen, eating an apple or sandwich, and sits on couch resting his feet on the coffee table. GLINDA dusts her way around TERRY and finally dusts his feet off the table. He rises and moves to the desk where he sits on the desk chair, opens the second drawer and uses it for a foot rest.*)

TERRY. Why are you dusting again?
GLINDA. A woman's work is never done.
TERRY. But you dusted yesterday.
GLINDA. Tell that to the *new* dust.
TERRY. But you hardly ever dust more than two-three times a week.
GLINDA. And don't think I haven't felt guilty about it!
TERRY. Guilt never bothered you before.
GLINDA. At my age, I prefer spending my hours with a clean conscience.
TERRY. Not to mention clean tables, clean lamps, clean walls . . .
GLINDA. Eat your apple (*sandwich*) it's getting dusty!
TERRY. You should get that spray stuff; it wouldn't throw up all those clouds.
GLINDA. (*pauses, extends duster*) Perhaps you'd like to show me the *proper* way?
TERRY. (*backs off*) No thanks. Don't want to lose my amateur standing.

GLINDA. That's what I figured. (*resumes dusting*)

TERRY. Seriously — why *are* you dusting again today?

GLINDA. (*pausing*) Too much time on my hands, all at once.

TERRY. You mean without *Dad* here to do for?

GLINDA. I *used* to spend this time of day fixing his *lunch*. But lately, well —

TERRY. He's home a *couple* of days a week.

GLINDA. It's not the same anymore. It's too random. I get out of phase.

TERRY. Why not use the extra time to make him an extra-special *dinner*, then?

GLINDA. I tried that. It doesn't work. When he shows up at dinnertime and I've just fixed lobster thermidor and asparagus with hollandaise, and he says, "That's what I had for lunch!", it kind of curdles my initiative.

TERRY. I *love* lobster thermidor! Does this mean I get nothing but drab dinners?

GLINDA. The trouble is, if I fix something fancy, and it's what he already had, then I have to fix him something *else*, and by the time that's finished, *my* dinner is *cold*!

TERRY. I see what you mean. How many lunches *is* it so far?

GLINDA. Today's Number Eight.

TERRY. Well, at least there's *one* nice benefit: Yolanda's *green* with envy of Miss Starr, spending so much time with Dad.

GLINDA. She won't be green *today*. It's *Miss Starr's* turn to pick the place. I just hope your father won't be *poisoned*!

TERRY. By Miss Starr?

GLINDA. By the *restaurant*! If *anyone* turns green today —

TERRY. —it'll be *Dad*!

(*BLACKOUT*)

Scene changes to HYMIE'S HASH HOUSE

LUNCH #8 – HYMIE'S HASH HOUSE
SETTING: *CHUCK and CHARITY are moving to a table in "HYMIE'S HASH HOUSE" and not too eagerly; they sit down, he picks up a menu very gingerly between tip of thumb-and-forefinger and then sets it flat on the table before him, and carefully brushes thumb-and-forefinger off on the tablecloth. Then:*

CHUCK. Nice place, if you're illiterate. You can tell what they have to offer by studying the stains on the menu.

CHARITY. Now, Mister Reynolds, at our last luncheon you *agreed* that *I* could select every-*other*-restaurant.

CHUCK. At the time, I thought you were sane.

CHARITY. Just because this room doesn't have fancy decor . . .

CHUCK. I didn't say that. I mean, that could be *imported* sawdust on the floor.

WAITER. (*arrives at tableside, a rumple-haired, tieless yahoo in a stained apron*) What'll it be?

CHARITY. What's today's special?

WAITER. Clean plates. (*laughs at his own joke*)

CHARITY. Besides that.

WAITER. (*shrugs*) *Hash!* (*points to sign*) What *else*?!

CHUCK. (*to CHARITY:*) Why don't *you* order for both of us? That way my death won't be a suicide.

CHARITY. (*to WAITER:*) What would *you* recommend?

WAITER. Another restaurant. (*laughs*)

CHUCK. Seriously.

WAITER. (*he leans down between them and, in a suddenly very solemn voice:*) Another restaurant. (*laughs again*)

CHARITY. You look familiar.

WAITER. I *could* be, if your boyfriend wasn't here.

CHUCK. I am *not* her boyfriend!

WAITER. (*cuddling up to CHARITY*) Well, lucky me!

CHARITY. (*pulling away*) This is a *business* luncheon.

WAITER. *Here*? Business must be *lousy*!

CHARITY. Look, let me put it this way: if you were eating here, what would you get?

WAITER. Ptomaine. (*laughs*)

CHUCK. You know, there *is* something familiar about you — do you have a *cousin* who waits tables at Chateau Jasper?

WAITER. Hey, that's my brother Larry! Our family comes from a long line of waiters.

CHUCK. I'm surprised it's not a long *unemployment* line!

WAITER. So are we! (*laughs*)

CHARITY. Listen, I don't have a very long lunch break. Let me try one last time: If somebody comes in here and doesn't want to try the hash, what do they get?

WAITER. The heave-ho.

CHUCK. I surrender. Two orders of hash.

WAITER. (*to CHARITY:*) And what'll *you* have? (*laughs at own joke*) Sorry. That's waiter humor. (*as he Exits*) I kill me!

CHARITY. (*after a pause*) I'm *sure* the food'll be just fine. I mean, they couldn't *operate* this place without a license from the Board of Health.

CHUCK. What makes you think the Board of Health would even set foot in this *neighborhood*?

CHARITY. I suppose it — it is just a bit more degenerate than I thought it'd be. But that accountant on our paper gets so *awfully* suspicious of everyone's expense accounts.

CHUCK. Well, don't worry about it. You probably won't live long enough to turn one in.

WAITER. (*arrives at tableside, sets two plates before them*) Two orders of Hymie's hash. Can I get you anything else?

CHUCK. (*after a look at his plate, raises a hopeful glance to the Waiter*) Two orders of the antidote?

WAITER. As soon as medical science discovers one. (*laughs, Exits*)

CHARITY. Well — *bon appetit*!

CHUCK. Don't you mean "*bon voyage*"?

CHARITY. We've got to at least try it. If we didn't, the chef would be offended.

CHUCK. And that bothers you? (*prods hash with tip of fork*) I wonder what kind of meat this is, anyway?

CHARITY. If you don't mind, I'd rather not think about it. (*nervously lifts fork to lips but doesn't taste*)

CHUCK. You're going to have to give the paramedics *some* kind of clue!

CHARITY. (*sets down forkful, speaks almost in tears*) But I'm *hungry*! And I have to get back to the office in another fifteen minutes, and I can't work on an empty stomach!

CHUCK. What makes you think if you eat this stuff that your stomach won't empty *itself*?

CHARITY. (*stands*) This is never going to work! We're spending much too much time talking about food, or the service, or — When do we get down to playwriting-lessons?

CHUCK. Right now. Sit.

CHARITY. What?

CHUCK. Sit, and we'll plunge right into the lesson.

CHARITY. (*after a moment, sits*) Okay, teacher. Lay it on me.

CHUCK. The first thing a good playwright does is *observe* the world around him. Why, you could almost write down everything we've been saying here and make an entire *scene* out of it. Can you imagine an audience *not* being fascinated by that *waiter* of ours?

CHARITY. I—I never thought of that.

CHUCK. Well, *think* about it. Observe, study and *store* every single thing that ever happens to you! Then, when you get to your typewriter—get it all down!

CHARITY. But it's all so kind of—disjointed . . . random . . . helter-skelter. Where's the *wrapup*?

CHUCK. That's where your *craft* comes in. Link it up, smooth it out, cut away the excess parts, until you have something that'll make people sit up and pay attention!

WAITER. (*rushes to tableside*) Look, maybe you two better go, Hymie's getting real upset.

CHUCK/CHARITY. What?

WAITER. He can hear everything you've been saying, back in the kitchen—"Get it all down!" . . . "Kind of disjointed!" . . . "Cut away the excess parts!"

CHARITY. But it's all a mistake. We weren't *talking* about his *hash*.

WAITER. It's too late for apologies. You've broken Hymie's heart.

CHUCK. Maybe if we sent "our compliments to the chef" . . . ?

WAITER. (*folds his arms*) He won't believe you unless you eat something first!

CHARITY. (*stands*) There's no time. I've got to get back to the office. Would it help heal his heart if we asked for a couple of Doggy Bags —?

WAITER. (*leans closer, conspiratorily*) I wouldn't recommend it.

CHUCK. Why not?

WAITER. I like dogs. (*laughs*)

CHUCK. (*Stands, takes CHARITY by the arm, while handing a $10 bill to Waiter.*) And *you* said there wasn't any *wrapup*!

WAITER. (*pocketing bill*) Thank you, sir! Come again, anytime!

CHARITY. (*as CHUCK starts leading her out of restaurant*) But *I'm* supposed to pay for lunch!

CHUCK. Save your money for tomorrow — at The Four Seasons!

(*CHARITY gives him a look of financial terror as they Exit, during:*)

WAITER. If you see my brother Louie there, tell him Percival says "Hi".

CHUCK/CHARITY. (*stop short of Exit*) "Percival"?

WAITER. (*shrugs*) I was a lot luckier than my brother *Evelyn*!

BLACKOUT

(*Living room. GLINDA and TERRY on sofa, watching (screen unseen by us) television. TERRY's munching on apple. Sound of gunshots, galloping horses, etc. DOORBELL rings. GLINDA gets up.*)

GLINDA. Turn that thing down, will you? (*heads for front door*) Our caller might be the sort who sues for shattered eardrums. (*TERRY picks up remote control and reduces volume at same time as GLINDA opens front door and YOLANDA steps in; GLINDA turns and observes to TERRY.*) I was right!

YOLANDA. (*striking a pose against the doorjamb*) Is Chucky home?

TERRY. *We'll* never tell!

GLINDA. Terry! (*then, to YOLANDA:*) I'm sorry, but Mister Reynolds is lunching in Manhattan today.

YOLANDA. He seems to lunch out a *lot* lately. Maybe he doesn't like the way you *cook*. I haven't seen him for at least ten days.

TERRY. Maybe he doesn't like the way *you* cook!

YOLANDA. (*missing his extra meaning—though GLINDA's glare at TERRY shows that* she *didn't*) I've *never* cooked for Chucky!

TERRY. I never had a doubt about that.

GLINDA. Terry, go someplace and do something! (*TERRY shrugs, Exits to kitchen chomping his apple.*)

YOLANDA. Isn't all that lunching in town rather *expensive* for Miss Starr's newspaper budget?

TERRY. (*off*) It sure is *today*! The Four Seasons costs an arm and a leg just to use their *water* glasses!

YOLANDA. (*elated*) The Four Seasons! Lunches there last *ever* so long. Maybe I can *catch* him! (*turns and Exits, fast*)

GLINDA. (*to TERRY, just re-entering room:*) *Now* see what your big mouth has done!

TERRY. I sure hope Dad eats fast!

GLINDA. Me, too. After Hymie's Hash House we're all out of bicarbonate — and if he looks up and see *Yolanda* while he's eating . . . !

TERRY. (*gestures with apple*) *Please*, Glinda: *I'm* eating!

BLACKOUT – change to The Four Seasons

LUNCH #27 – THE FOUR SEASONS

SETTING: *CHUCK and CHARITY are seated at The Four Seasons by a waiter dressed in a tuxedo. As they are seated, the waiter hands them menus.*

CHARITY. At least in this restaurant I'll know what I'm eating.

CHUCK. By the way, how *did* you pick Hymie's Hash House?

CHARITY. Well, I just opened the yellow pages to the restaurant listings, closed my eyes and picked one at random.

CHUCK. Sort of a gastronomical Russian Roulette.

CHARITY. You've made your point. (*opens menu*) I'd rather pay a little more just to . . .

CHUCK. What's the matter?

CHARITY. (*Stage whisper*) This menu has no *prices* on it!

CHUCK. So? You expect a restaurant that was used for an instant coffee commercial to have prices on the menu?

CHARITY. Yes. How will I know how much the meal is?

CHUCK. The waiter gives you the bill.

CHARITY. But I'd like to know before I order. (*sees WAITER*) Excuse me . . .

WAITER. (*Comes to table*) Why? Did you spill something?

CHARITY. Waiter, there are no prices on the menu.

WAITER. OH, NO! There's a big mistake. You were given the menus with the invisible ink.

CHARITY. Well, we would like the menus with prices on them.

CHUCK. Mine will do.

WAITER. We usually only bring out these invisible ink menus when we have a Shriner's Convention. They get a real hoot out of it. (*takes menus and Exits*)

CHARITY. I knew there was a mistake.

CHUCK. These restaurants never have the prices on the menus.

CHARITY. But the waiter said . . .

CHUCK. He was putting you on. He probably thought you were a tourist. Besides, I don't think you want to know the prices before you eat.

CHARITY. I want to know before we *ORDER*.

CHUCK. No you don't. *Trust* me.

CHARITY. Why don't I want to know?

CHUCK. Because it's going to *ruin* your appetite. Haven't you ever eaten here before?

CHARITY. I came here on a date one time. But I didn't look at the menu. I let him order for both of us.

CHUCK. So you have no idea of the cost? Have you ever heard the term "sticker shock"?

CHARITY. But why would you . . . ?

CHUCK. It was my turn to pick the restaurant. Besides, I picked up the check at HYMIE'S.

WAITER. (*Enters with the new menus*) I am so sorry. I shall make sure the Maitre D is flogged (*Hands menu to CHARITY who stares in disbelief.*)

CHUCK. You're Louie, right?

WAITER. Have we met before?

CHUCK. No, but Percival says "HI".

WAITER. Where did you see Percival?

CHUCK. He waited on us at HYMIE'S.

WAITER. And you're out of the hospital already? (*pause*) How *does* it feel to have your stomach pumped?

CHUCK. We didn't wait for the special.

WAITER. They were having clean plates?

CHUCK. (*to CHARITY:*) Are you ready to order? (*No response. He pulls down her menu. She is in a trance from the shock of the prices.*)

WAITER. She's paying, right?

CHUCK. How could you tell?

WAITER. Oh, it happens all the time . . . but usually when they see the *bill.*

CHUCK. You'd better alert the nearest Cardiac Care Center.

WAITER. She'll be fine.

CHUCK. Not after I order.

WAITER. Oh boy!

CHUCK. Bring us a bottle of your finest domestic champagne. (*turns to CHARITY*) Is that all right with you? (*No response – still staring at menu. Then to WAITER*) Must be fine with her. (*WAITER Exits. To CHARITY:*) Miss Starr? (*No response*) Miss Starr? (*No response*) Charity? (*Dips fingertips into water glass and flicks water onto CHARITY's face*)

CHARITY. (*finally responding*) What happened?

CHUCK. I tried to *warn* you about the prices.

CHARITY. This meal could cost more than the gross national product of several third world countries.

CHUCK. What difference should it make to you? The paper's paying.

CHARITY. I *hope.* If the accountant doesn't approve the charges, it'll take me *years* to repay. Have you ever heard the phrase *indentured servitude*?

CHUCK. Why worry about it now? Have you decided what you're going to order?

CHARITY. I've got no appetite. (*WAITER returns with ice bucket, two glasses and champagne which is already opened.*) What's this?

CHUCK. Champagne. I asked you if it was all right. You never objected.

WAITER. I took the liberty of uncorking the champagne in the wine closet. Loud noises have a tendency to disturb our customers.

CHARITY. (*looking around*) Everyone looks so stiff and sullen.

CHUCK. Probably have menus with the prices on them.

WAITER. (*pouring champagne*) Are you ready to order yet? I really was hoping to squeeze in working on my car's transmission.

CHARITY. Who are you trying to kid? Your car can't be here; there's nowhere to park it.

WAITER. I never said my car was here. I figured I might have enough time to take a taxi to Jersey, repair the transmission and take a taxi back.

CHUCK. Were you and your brothers graduates of the Don Rickles School of Waiter Etiquette?

WAITER. No. We come by this charm naturally. It's a gift.

CHUCK. Like two heads.

WAITER. Clever.

CHUCK. I know what I want. (*to CHARITY:*) Are you sure you're not hungry?

CHARITY. I'll just have some champagne.

CHUCK. You really shouldn't drink on an empty stomach.

CHARITY. Believe me, if I did eat, I'd have an empty stomach after I saw the bill. I'd rather keep the status quo. (*takes a drink*)

CHUCK. What ever you say. (*to WAITER:*) I'll start out with the escargot for an appetizer. Then I'll have the bibb lettuce salad with the special house dressing and then I'll have the stuffed sole florentine.

WAITER. Very nice choice. (*Exits*)

CHARITY. Once I get the bill for this, I may never

regain my appetite again. (*drinks*)

CHUCK. Today's lesson will be worth the cost of the meal. We are going to discuss conflict (*drinks*) as it relates to plot development.

CHARITY. I *hope* this is worth all these lunches. I'm really eager to learn.

CHUCK. If there is anything that is essential to a good play, it is conflict. In order to keep your audience's attention, you must have CONFLICT.

YOLANDA. (o.s.) Yoo hoo! (*Enters with WAITER*) Well, *Chucky*! What are you doing *here*? I haven't seen much of you lately.

CHUCK. Well, between my playwriting and helping Miss Starr learn playwriting, I just haven't been too accessible.

YOLANDA. I'll say you haven't! I hope you don't mind if I join you. I just hate eating alone.

CHUCK. I'm sure Miss Starr won't mind. (*to WAITER:*) Bring us another chair and another glass, and, oh yes, another menu. (*WAITER Exits.*)

YOLANDA. (*to CHARITY:*) Isn't he just the sweetest thing? I mean you're so mean and nasty to poor Chucky, and he is so forgiving. He is willing to take you out to lunch and teach you about writing plays. (*WAITER returns with menu and glass and pours champagne. YOLANDA moves between CHUCK and CHARITY and settles on the edge of CHARITY's chair. To CHARITY*) You don't mind, do you? (*concentrating on CHUCK again*) He is really a dear! (*CHUCK's attention is now drawn to YOLANDA.*) Chucky, you order for me please. (*CHARITY is really getting upset and gives up her chair, standing behind it as YOLANDA takes over.*) Now you two just go on like I wasn't here. What were you talking about before I interrupted?

CHUCK. *Conflict!* (*to WAITER:*) We're going to need a second bottle of champagne!

(*CHARITY begins to loose control behind YOLANDA.*)

BLACKOUT

(*Living Room. GLINDA's in the desk chair, reading a novel. TERRY's sitting on the sofa, reading a comic book; he sighs.*)

GLINDA. Batman in trouble again?

TERRY. No, I was just trying to remember what Dad's *face* looks like! Remember Dad?

GLINDA. Vaguely. A *tall* man, I think. Or was that Abraham Lincoln?

TERRY. (*with new enthusiasm*) You *remember* Abraham Lincoln?

GLINDA. Actually, I remember Raymond Massey. For all I know, Lincoln was built like Richard Simmons.

TERRY. I can't picture Honest Abe doing aerobics. Not without nausea.

GLINDA. Yours or Abe's?

TERRY. Take your pick. (*starts to read comic book again, then looks up*) How many lunches is it *now*?

GLINDA. I think today's is number forty-two. I wish I knew how the two of them stay so *slim* with all their daily gorging!

TERRY. Easy. After ever restaurant *Charity* picks, they both throw up! It's built-in bulemia.

GLINDA. Whose turn is it today?

TERRY. Charity's

GLINDA. (*rises, starts for kitchen*) I'd better put bicarbonate on my shopping list.

BLACKOUT. Change to KALI'S KOSHER KITCHEN

LUNCH #42 – KALI'S KOSHER KITCHEN
SETTING: *We find CHUCK and CHARITY seated at the table in "KALI'S KOSHER KITCHEN", a pseudo-*Indian *emporium (the New Delhi, not Choctaw-type) with maybe an "ambience-item" or two on the table; they are studying their menus:*

CHUCK. Don't they have any flavoring but *curry* in this place?

CHARITY. It's an *Indian* restaurant. What did you expect?

CHUCK. I'm not sure. The "kosher" part kind of threw me.

CHARITY. Maybe the proprietor's half-Indian and half-Jewish. It wouldn't make much difference, food-wise.

CHUCK. Why not?

CHARITY. Well, the Hindus don't eat beef, and the Moslems and Jews don't eat pork, so it shouldn't be too difficult keeping things kosher, curry or not.

CHUCK. That explains why everything seems to be *lamb.* Whoever wrote "Mary had a little lamb" obviously didn't come from Calcutta!

CHARITY. Well, he didn't say "has" a little lamb; it *is* in the *past tense.*

CHUCK. (*improvising*) "It followed her to school one day, which was against the rule, and so the children had a gay lamb cookout at the school!"

CHARITY. Actually, the "kosher" doesn't bother me as much as the "Kali" part. Isn't she the goddess of doom and destruction, like in that Indiana Jones movie?

CHUCK. If you *knew* that, why did you *pick* this place?

CHARITY. The food is supposed to be *authentic.* Just what the people in India eat.

CHUCK. Have you ever seen *photographs* of the people in India? They all seem to be starving. Though, judging by this menu, I don't *blame* them.

CHARITY. Don't be such a chicken. American food is so boring. You should give your taste-buds a new experience.

CHUCK. Yes, but must it be a *fatal* one?

CHARITY. Come on, now. There must be *something* that appeals to you.

CHUCK. Well — maybe this lamb-kebab thing. I suspect it'll be mostly vegetables and rice. In small doses, the meat might not destroy our alimentary canals.

CHARITY. That looks good to me, too. Let's *both* get it. (*sets down menu*)

CHUCK. (*setting down menu*) I never said it looked *good* — just least worst.

CHARITY. I wonder what's keeping our waiter?

CHUCK. He's probably having his *own* lunch somewhere *else.*

CHARITY. No, wait. Here he comes.

WAITER. (*Enters wearing turban, brocade vest, silken sash, pantaloons, and sandals with turned-up toes.*) Are the sahib and memsahib ready to order?

CHUCK. Ready as we'll *ever* be.

CHARITY. We'll have the lamb-kebobs, please.

WAITER. Regular or hot?

CHUCK. What's the difference?

WAITER. The regular comes with icewater; the hot comes with a fire extinguisher.

CHARITY. We'll have the regular. Food that's *too* spicy-hot is hard to *taste.*

CHUCK. Of course, that could be a *mercy.*

WAITER. (*to CHARITY:*) The sahib has a point.

CHARITY. Perhaps you have a *slightly*-hotter-than-regular version?

WAITER. I'll check with Jawaharlal.

CHUCK. Who's that?

WAITER. Our cook and owner: Jawaharlal Feinberg.

CHARITY. (*to CHUCK:*) There! What'd I tell you?! (*to WAITER:*) So the meat really *is* kosher.

WAITER. Mostly. Of course, some days the rabbi can't get over here to kill it.

CHUCK. And what then?

WAITER. (*mysteriously*) We . . . make do.

CHARITY. (*doesn't like the sound of this*) How do you mean? The meat is —*fresh*, isn't it?

WAITER. Of course!

CHUCK. You're sure —?

WAITER. (*as Exits*) Have I ever lied to you? (*a moment later, from offstage, we hear a plaintive sound of* "Maaaa . . . Maaaa!" *followed by a* gunshot *and* thud; *CHARITY stands wordlessly, her face mournful, and half-turns to depart; CHUCK takes her hand and stops her*)

CHUCK. Charity —you *asked* for *fresh* . . .

CHARITY. (*after a second, sits again slowly*) Not *that* fresh!

CHUCK. (*retains hold on her hand, pats it gently*) I'm sure the poor creature didn't *suffer* . . . (*then we hear a louder* "MAAA . . . MAAAAA!" *followed by another* gunshot *then* another *then* another . . . *and then a heartbreaking, dwindling* "MAAAAAaaaaaa . . . " *and a* very *loud* thud)

CHARITY. (*after an exquisite pause*) . . . you were saying?

CHUCK. (*uneasily*) It's not as if we didn't *know* getting meat involves the slaughter of animals . . .

CHARITY. True. I just didn't expect to be an accomplice.

WAITER. (*arrives at tableside*) There's been a slight delay. The kebobs you ordered will take about twenty minutes longer than we figured.

CHARITY. (*sincerely*) The longer the better. I couldn't quite *face* those little kebobs right now.

WAITER. It's not as bad as you think. Wait 'til *later* today when the *kids* come home from school.

CHUCK. What kids? (*Pause. CHUCK and CHARITY react.*) The *lamb's*?

WAITER. *My* kids. The lamb was their *pet.* (*CHUCK and CHARITY both come to their feet now.*)

CHARITY. You're joking!

WAITER. It even had a *name.*

CHUCK. I don't want to hear any more!

WAITER. Its name was "Woolie"!

CHARITY. (*fumbling with her purse*) How much do we owe you?

WAITER. It had a cute little red bow around its neck. (*dangles ribbon he's been hiding in closed hand*)

CHUCK. *Stop,* already!

WAITER. The kids were trying to teach it to roll over.

CHARITY. (*thrusting a fistful of bills into the WAITER's hand*) Please!

WAITER. It just learned *how.*

CHUCK. Sorry, we've got to run! (*He and CHARITY start out.*)

WAITER. Thank you! Come again!

CHARITY. (*to CHUCK as they Exit.*) But what about today's *playwriting* lesson —?

CHUCK. Well, I *was* going to teach you how to create a

mood of *terror* onstage – but *now* I think that would be kind of *superfluous*!

CHARITY. *Amen!*

BLACKOUT

(*LIVING ROOM. GLINDA and TERRY are seated side by side on the sofa, staring into space. They hold this pose for at least a count of five; then, not even looking at each other throughout dialog:*)

TERRY. What day is today?

GLINDA. Lunch Number fifty-eight.

TERRY. I mean in *real* time.

GLINDA. I don't know. Tuesday? Wednesday? It doesn't seem to matter any more.

TERRY. Do I have school today?

GLINDA. Who cares?!

TERRY. Will Dad skip lunch for my graduation?

GLINDA. Who knows?!

TERRY. I do still *have* a Dad, don't I?

GLINDA. Who remembers?!

TERRY. Which one picks the restaurant today?

GLINDA. They're lunching at Wally's Wiener World. Does that give you a clue?

TERRY. Our bank account must be down below zero by now.

GLINDA. I don't see how. Charity's paying for all the lunches.

TERRY. But *we're* paying for the *bicarbonate*!

GLINDA. Not any more. Your father's moved up to Pepto-Bismol.

TERRY. Does it come with two straws?

GLINDA. (*finally looks at TERRY*) You think he'd *share* with Charity?

TERRY. (*looks at GLINDA*) I'm not sure — but lately, when he's getting dressed to go to meet her — he *hums* a lot!

GLINDA. You don't suppose — ?

TERRY. A playwright and a theatre critic? It'd be a *first* —

GLINDA. But would it *last*?!

TERRY. Of course, she *has* got great legs . . .

GLINDA. But after Wally's Wiener World will she be able to *stand* on them?

TERRY. Maybe we should have *told* Yolanda where they'll be today. If she joined them *there* —

GLINDA. (*nods*) — it would serve her right! But we gave our solemn oath we'd never reveal his lunchtime whereabouts again.

TERRY. At Wally's Wiener World he might make an exception.

GLINDA. It can't be *that* bad, can it?

TERRY. With that newspaper accountant breathing down Charity's neck?

GLINDA. You're right. We *should* have told Yolanda!

BLACKOUT
LUNCH#50 – WALLY'S WIENER WORLD

SETTING: *CHUCK and CHARITY are seating themselves at Wally's Wiener World. Charity is carrying a folder. On the table are containers of ketchup, mustard, onions and relish.*

CHUCK. How do you keep *finding* these places?!

CHARITY. You mean these places with *character*?

CHUCK. No, I mean these places that look like the dining room at Alcatraz.

CHARITY. But, don't you remember what you said about observing the great *characters* these waiters are?

CHARITY. So *that's* why we've been coming to these little out-of-the-way spots! *I* thought it was because you were *cheap*.

CHARITY. The waiters at *your* places are plastic and rude and snooty.

CHUCK. The waiters at *your* places look like they escaped from Devil's Island.

(*WAITER Enters. He is dressed in greasy T-shirt and apron. Cigar is dangling out of his mouth; he has a knife in his hand.*)

WAITER. (*in gruff voice*) What's that?

CHUCK/CHARITY. (*turn around, startled*) NOTHING!

CHARITY. (*panic-stricken*) May we see a menu?

WAITER. A what?

CHARITY. A *menu*. May we see a *menu*?

WAITER. Whatsamatter? Can't you read the *wall*?

(*CHUCK & CHARITY both look at the wall placard behind their table*)

CHARITY. The letters keep moving.

WAITER. What? Those ain't letters. (*Grabs her folder from the table and crosses to wall and swats at flies, watching one fly away. Crosses back and returns folder to table. CHUCK and CHARITY react in disgust to the return of folder*) Now, whatcha want?

CHARITY. We'd like a minute or two to decide. *Please?*

WAITER. Well, hurry up! I can't keep 'em off the wall all day. Besides, I might git another customer.

CHUCK. I doubt it.

WAITER. (*gruffly*) What's that?

CHARITY. Just give us some time. (*WAITER Exits.*)

CHUCK. You *really* picked a place this time! This even beats *Hymie's*!

CHARITY. Let's get out of here while we can. We can go to one of *your* places no matter what the cost.

CHUCK. Maybe we can sneak out of here before he comes back. (*CHARITY gingerly removes pages from folder. They stand and start to back out opposite waiter's Exit. WAITER Enters behind them*)

WAITER. Where ya goin'?

CHARITY. *Us?* (*CHUCK and CHARITY move closer to wall*) We were just . . . uh . . .

CHUCK. Going to take a closer look at your magical moving menu wall!

WAITER. OH. (*seem satisfied*) So, whatcha want?

CHUCK. (*Stares at the wall.*) I'll have a *DIRTY HARRY DOG*..

WAITER. Very good choice.

CHUCK. What *is* a *DIRTY HARRY DOG*?

WAITER. That's one of Wally's famous wieners which you can cover with as much (*mock stab in his own heart with knife*) ketchup as ya' want.

CHUCK. Sounds delicious.

CHARITY. What's the *DAYS OF OUR LIVES DOG*?

WAITER. That's one of Wally's famous wieners which ya' can cover with as many (*mock tears down face gesture with hand*) onions as ya' want.

CHUCK. Then your breath could match your reviews.

CHARITY. (*Ignoring him.*) What about the *GRETA GARBO DOG*?

WAITER. That's one of Wally's famous wieners which ya' add nothing. (*very dramatic*) It wants to be alone! (*chuckles*) I shoulda been an actor!

CHARITY. Could I just have one with mustard and relish?

WAITER. That would be the *TOM CRUISE DOG*. That's one of Wally's famous wieners which ya' can cover with —

CHUCK/CHARITY. As much mustard and relish as you want.

CHUCK. And two beers. *Light* beers.

WAITER. We ain't got light beer.

CHUCK. We'll take whatever you have then.

CHARITY. You don't happen to be Wally, do you?

WAITER. Me? (*laughs*) Nah! I got waitin' in my blood. Come from a family of waiters . . . the name's *Evelyn*. (*Exits*)

CHARITY. I don't know what's scarier — risking getting Evelyn angry or eating in this place.

CHUCK. I choose eating. I don't want to get any guy named *Evelyn* angry.

CHARITY. You're right. Anyway, what could they do to a hot dog?

CHUCK. You *don't* want to know. I'm glad we didn't ask him what the *DIRTY DOG* was.

WAITER. (*Enters with beers*) Here's your brews. (*forces his way between them and pops the tabs, both at the same time, allowing spray to fly at will*)

CHARITY. (*with a forced smile*) Thanks.

WAITER. BON APPETITE! (*pronounced "BON-AP-A-TIT-EE" LAUGHS AS EXITS.*)

CHARITY. (*mimicking waiter's pronunciation*) You know what Bon Appetite means?

CHUCK. Isn't that a French company that makes stomach pumps?

CHARITY. I'm ready to get down to business. (*carefully removes papers from folder and sorts through them*) I've got my character descriptions, my plot outline, samples of dialogue, flow chart showing the sequence of the action, ground plan, costume and property lists. Plus other things you asked for. (*hands pile of papers to him*)

CHUCK. Sounds to me like you're ready to write. (*starts to browse through papers*) I'll look these over tonight and when we meet tomorrow I'll get you on your way to be the first playwright from the Charlton Reynolds Famous Playwright's school.

(*WAITER Enters. Carries buns in arm pit. CHUCK & CHARITY react. WAITER removes buns from under arm.*)

WAITER. A little bun warmer. You like that? (*sets down buns on table and takes hot dogs out of apron pocket and slaps them on bun.* [*NOTE: Premiere's apron had center pocket-neck strap and top of apron was left down over pocket so that it became a "production" to produce the hot dogs, one at a time.*] *CHUCK & CHARITY observe this ritual in stunned disbelief*)

CHARITY. If we don't die of ptomaine first.

BLACKOUT

(*LIVING ROOM – TERRY has school books, is crossing toward door, stops as GLINDA Enters, in light topcoat and carrying purse.*)

TERRY. Did Dad get off okay?

GLINDA. Well, he got onto the train. Now it's up to the Long Island Railroad. (*will divest self of coat and purse during*) Funny thing, though . . .

TERRY. What?

GLINDA. There was this *woman* down at the far end of the platform . . .

TERRY. What's funny about *that*?

GLINDA. She looked an *awful* lot like *Yolanda*!

TERRY. But you're not *sure*?

GLINDA. It was too crowded to go and check her out. Besides, with her coat-collar turned up, and that heavy veil on her hat covering her face, I couldn't do a positive I.D.

TERRY. Did you tell Dad?

GLINDA. He'd already boarded by then. And *she* got aboard before I could push my way through the crowd of commuters.

TERRY. Maybe I'd better skip school today and ride into town and *warn* him!

GLINDA. (*points toward front door*) Don't miss your bus.

TERRY. Aw!

GLINDA. Besides, you'd never get into Pierre's Palais de Pompe.

TERRY. They don't admit kids?

GLINDA. They don't admit *anybody* who looks like he doesn't have collateral for a house-loan!

TERRY. Then *today* must be *Dad's* turn to pick!

GLINDA. I'm not sure. Did you know that, for awhile now, *he's* been paying for every other lunch?

TERRY. And he's really humming up a *storm* these days, too.

GLINDA. Don't be ridiculous!

TERRY. Glinda, *you* just don't appreciate the Power of Positive Great Legs! (*Exits*)

BLACKOUT

LUNCH#77 – PIERRE'S PALAIS DE POMPE

SETTING: *We find CHUCK and CHARITY already seated at an elegant table in "Pierre's Palais de Pompe". They don't realize it—but we notice— that their antagonism is now a thing of the past, and they are obviously Two Good Friends enjoying one another's company, and very much on a first name basis besides; in fact, they're In Love, but don't know it yet; WAITER Enters with cocktail tray and gives them their after-dinner drinks on his line:*)

WAITER. Courvoisier for M'sieu, and Benedictine for M'am'selle!

CHUCK. *Merci bien, François.*

WAITER. Will there be anything else, M'sieu?

CHUCK. Just *l'addition, s'il vous plait.*

WAITER. *Toute de suite, M'sieu!* (*Exits*)

CHARITY. Why do the French call the bill "the addition"? At *these* prices, it should be, the "*multiplication*"!

CHUCK. You gotta admit the food was just *great*, though. A little hard to *recognize* under all those different *sauces*, but whatever I had for lunch, it was luscious!

CHARITY. Same here! Now, let's get down to business: Chuck, I owe you an apology.

CHUCK. For what, Char? (*pronounced "chair" as a truncation of her name*)

CHARITY. Those *terrible* things I said in my review of your play. Until you started teaching me about playwriting, I never *realized* that characters in a mystery simply *have* to be two-dimensional.

CHUCK. (*takes her hand*) I'll never so much as mention your rotten review again. (*both laugh*) I have a confession. Originally, I had no intention whatsoever of being helpful to you—I was angry—I wanted to bleed you with high prices, and teach you *nothing* of value to a playwright. But then — then suddenly — meeting you got to be so much fun that — that — (*now he's subdued*) well, it got to be fun.

CHARITY. (*squeezing their still-clasped hands with her free hand*) Did it ever!

CHUCK. (*grins*) You took the words right out of my mouth! (*over-clasps the three hands with his remaining hand; then, impishly, she pulls her hand from the bottom of the pile and places it on the top; he abruptly does the same thing; and then they are paying a frantic one-hand-over-the-other "one-upsmanship" like happy kids as the WAITER returns with the bill; BOTH see him simultaneously, and they immediately sit back in feigned high-class decorum*)

WAITER. Would you like a flyswatter?

CHUCK. (*guiltily*) I guess it *did* look like a *bug*-squashing binge, but we were only — only — (*to CHARITY, sincerely blank:*) What *is* that hand-stacking thing called, anyway?

WAITER. *Gauche, m'sieu!* (*hands him the folder containing the bill*) *L'addition.*

CHUCK. (*takes it*) Thank you. I mean, *merci.*

WAITER. (*replying bilingually*) You're welcome. I mean, *pas de quoi.*

CHARITY. Chuck, I think the reason the man is still *standing* there is that he now expects you to *pay* the bill!

CHUCK. Oh, yeah, sure! (*Starts to reach into his inner jacket pocket, then shakes his head in chagrin, and tenders folder to CHARITY.*) My mistake. This one's on *you!*

CHARITY. (*reacts*) It is? But — it *can't* be!

CHUCK. Why can't it?

CHARITY. Because this is a *Monday* on an *even*-numbered day of the month! *Your* treat. (*hands the folder back to him*)

CHUCK. No-no, *I* paid for the *last* lunch, remember? So *this* one's on *you.* (*returns folder to her*)

CHARITY. Yes, but *my* luncheon was supposed to have been last *Saturday,* but I had to cover that unexpected matinee-benefit and we had to cancel, remember? So now it's *your* turn again.

CHUCK. How *can* it be? If you didn't *take* your turn, then this is *still* your turn!

CHARITY. But you *always* get the odd-numbered Mondays!

CHARITY. Not *this* time, honey! Your matinee-reviewing shifted our schedule!

WAITER. (*who has been looking back and forth from one to the other in icy disinterest*) Perhaps I should retire discreetly from the battlefield for a moment. Meanwhile, you might just consider *tossing a coin!* (*Exits with a snobbish aplomb*)

CHARITY. Chuck, if I were you I'd *stiff* him on the *tip* for his smart-mouth attitude.

CHUCK. You mean *you* should stiff him on the tip, *don't* you?

CHARITY. (*with an abashed smile*) Actually, thinking this was *your* treat today, I didn't bring along any *money!*

CHUCK. (*slightly stunned*) *You either* . . . ?!

CHARITY. (*reacts to the import of his words*) Oh, Chuck! You don't mean . . . ?!

CHUCK. Not a penny. Well, wait, actually I have a *few* bucks in my pocket—but *this* bill is big enough for a down-payment on a *house!*

CHARITY. How about credit cards?

CHUCK. I usually carry American Express—but I left home without it!

CHARITY. Do you think they'd put the bill on my *Bloomingdale's* charge?

CHUCK. Damn, this is embarrassing! For *both* of us. How can we *explain* to that waiter — ?!

CHARITY. You know, Chuck — this is poetic justice, in a way. Until a month ago, when you said you'd feel better if we alternated paying for the lunches, besides picking out the restaurant, I would never have considered coming to a place this expensive. But then a greedy little voice deep down inside said, "Why *not*! Make *him* shell out for a change!" And this is my reward. I deserve it. (*she takes his hand, fondly, and he gently pats it*)

CHUCK. It's just as much my fault. When I figured your *newspaper* was picking up the tab, I decided to *splurge* a bit — always wanted to see the inside of this establishment — people said dining out here was unforgettable!

CHARITY. I know *I'll* never forget it! Chuck, what *are* we going to do about this bill?

CHUCK. We could leave something as collateral, maybe, till we got back with the cash —

CHARITY. Such as what? Belts? Shoes? Underwear?

CHUCK. Well, then, I guess we just throw ourselves on his mercy. Do you think he *has* any?

CHARITY. Him?! He'll probably run into the lobby shouting for the *gendarmes*!

CHUCK. Next thing, you and I will be in every paper in town, cheerily waving our handcuffs.

CHARITY. Oh, no, not in the papers! If my *office* found out where I was — !

CHUCK. Isn't this your lunch hour?

CHARITY. Not today. I had another matinee to cover, but didn't want to cancel lunch twice in a row, so I — well —

CHUCK. You *skipped* the performance?! Charity, how will you write your *review*?

CHARITY. I'll use Pauline's notes.

CHUCK. Your kid sister? *She's* covering the matinee for you?!

CHARITY. (*defensively*) Well, she *is* majoring in *journalism*!

CHUCK. Charity, your sister is *fourteen years old*!

CHARITY. It's a very progressive high school!

CHUCK. Well, that settles it! We've got to *sneak* out of here without paying!

CHARITY. (*a gleeful conspirator*) Do you think we can? I've never *done* that before in my *life*!

CHUCK. The trouble is, François is between us and the Exit.

CHARITY. Are there any windows in the men's washroom? There's an attendant in the ladies.

CHUCK. And a towel-seller in the men's.

CHARITY. Oh, Chuck, what in the world are we going to *do* . . . ?

(*Then BOTH react — and perk up — as they hear.*)

YOLANDA. Yoo-hoo! Chucky! (*YOLANDA Enters and CHUCK rises.*)

CHUCK. Why Yolanda. What a pleasant surprise. Did you slip a tracking-beeper into my coat-lining, or just rent a bloodhound for the afternoon?

YOLANDA. (*laughs*) If you *must* know — I followed you.

CHARITY. From Long Island?

YOLANDA. No, from your newspaper, Miss Starr. I happened to see Chuck pick you up there —

CHUCK. I *met* her there.

CHARITY. He did *not* pick me up!

YOLANDA. Whatever, Anyhow, I was just, oh, curious about where you two were having *this* day's "business meeti. ⊊" (*she makes it sound very unwholesome*) and after waiting outside for awhile, I got kind of *hungry*, so I just sashayed on in—

CHARITY. You *what* on in?

CHUCK. "Sashayed"; it's kind of a middle ground between "traipse" and "mosey".

CHARITY. (*comes to her feet; CHUCK is still on his*) Look, I have to go to the lady's room, so why don't you two sit down and have a nice cozy chat—

CHUCK. Funny coincidence, *I* have to go to the *men's* room. But Yolanda—(*gallantly pulls out chair, and she sits with pleasure*)—why don't you join us for an after-dinner drink?

YOLANDA. Why, *thank* you Chucky! I will!

CHUCK. (*taking CHARITY by the elbow and steering her off*) Your waiter's name is François; just wave that little folder at him and he'll come running.

CHARITY. (*to CHUCK*, sotto voce:) I'll race you to the elevator!

CHUCK. (*to CHARITY, similarly:*) Winner gets a wet kiss!

(*Both abruptly* gallop *off, hand-in-hand, passing a returning WAITER, who looks after them suspiciously, but who cannot resist YOLANDA eagerly waving the check-folder; he stops at tableside, takes folder.*)

WAITER. Are you ready to pay, *ma'am'selle*?

YOLANDA. (*pointing after fleeing duo*) Oh, *I'm* with *them*!

WAITER. (*peeks at amount of check, looks after them, then back at her—showing her the total bill inside the folder.*) You mean you *wish* you were.

(*YOLANDA does a gape-jawed "take" at amount; Both hold pose for three seconds; then:*)

BLACKOUT.

LIVING ROOM: GLINDA looking out window as TERRY Enters.

TERRY. Still not home?

GLINDA. (*turns back into room*) Well, he *did* phone to say he'd be just a *little* bit late, today. But I didn't think he'd miss *dinner*. How's the homework?

TERRY. All done. Thought I'd watch TV.

GLINDA. Don't you have a book report to write?

TERRY. Have to *read* the book first.

GLINDA. Well—?

TERRY. It's *Coningsby*, by Benjamin Disraeli. The life of a British schoolboy. *All* of it.

GLINDA. (*after a pause, moves to TV controller and turns on TV*) I'll see what's on TV. (*As she picks up TV Guide, doorbell rings; she replaces magazine, starts for the door.*) Now, *who* in the world—

TERRY. Maybe Dad forgot his key.

GLINDA. Door's not locked. He'd come right in. (*Opens door and YOLANDA, dressed as we last saw her, but carrying topcoat and hat with veil, strides angrily in; GLINDA closes door after her, then turns and remarks drily.*) Won't you come in?

YOLANDA. (*seething with rancor and pacing around room, looking in doorways*) Wherrrrrre is he?!

TERRY. (*innocently*) Where's who?

GLINDA. Do you mean Mister Reynolds?

YOLANDA. You know very well whom I mean! Thanks to him, I almost went to *jail*!

TERRY. On what charge?

YOLANDA. (*icily angry*) He and that *Starr* woman stuck *me* with their lunch-bill at the Palais de Pompe! And that loathsome waiter wouldn't believe they were coming back. And I said they surely would! (*in choked, weepy, little-girl voice:*) But they didn't! (*moves to chair and sits, voice icy again:*) And the bill was enough money to finance a car! And the waiter said he would turn the matter over to the police, and I panicked and ran, and he chased me for five blocks down the avenue, and a policeman grabbed me, so of course I had to say I was running from a purse-snatcher, and then the policeman chased the waiter *back* up the avenue, but his partner hung onto my purse as evidence, so I had to dodge away in the crowd and *hitchhike* back out onto Long Island, and when I see your father I'm going to *murder* him!

(*TERRY and GLINDA are having a hard time not laughing; they feign sympathy:*)

GLINDA. Won't the police be able to trace you from the contents of your purse?

YOLANDA. I never carry any identification or credit cards in it. Because of purse-snatchers. Just a packet of Kleenex, my comb, lipstick, Life Savers, a few subway tokens, a small mirror, a paperback Harlequin Romance novel, an emery board, and a Manhattan street guide.

TERRY. *That* should make it easy to pick a purse-snatcher out of a police line-up: He'd be the one with the *hernia*!

YOLANDA. That *isn't* very funny!

TERRY. (*nods in agreement*) It needs work.

GLINDA. Listen, I'm sure there's just been some sort of mixup—?

YOLANDA. They did it on purpose. They were *laughing* as they left!

GLINDA. I'm sure there's some extremely simple explanation—

YOLANDA. (*rising, starting to pace again*) Oh, there is! I'm *sure* there is. It's that *woman*! *She* put him up to it. I know the type! That cruel smile, those calculating eyes, that mocking voice—

TERRY. Those great legs—

YOLANDA. Those great leg—(*icily*) I can see I'll be getting no sympathy *here*! (*starts for door*)

GLINDA. Oh, but we're really *very* sorry—!

YOLANDA. (*Turns, looks uncertainly at GLINDA's face; GLINDA cannot maintain her pose for more than a second, and abruptly turns away and not-quiet-stifles a snorting laugh; YOLANDA ices over even more.*) You people haven't heard the last of this! (*turns on her heel and Exits*)

TERRY. You shouldn't have laughed.

GLINDA. I couldn't help it. What I wouldn't have given to see that five-block gallop! (*then more soberly*) I didn't like that look in her eye, though. She means trouble.

TERRY. What kind of trouble? She'll certainly never dare go to the *police* about it. They probably have an APB out on her all over Manhattan.

GLINDA. Well, that's true enough, I guess. But even so—(*Phone rings; she answers it*) Hello? . . . Oh, Mister Reynolds! We were *wondering*—Oh, I see. Yes . . . Yes, sir. See you then. (*hangs up*) They took that round-the-island Manhattan tour-boat cruise, and the boat ran out of gas or something. They just debarked five minutes ago.

TERRY. I've heard of guys running out of gas on a *car*-date. Leave it to Dad to go *spectacular*!

GLINDA. Your father sounded *very* happy, considering the inconvenience.

TERRY. Was he humming?

GLINDA. Like a hummingbird.

TERRY. You don't suppose—?

GLINDA. Well—I'm beginning to . . .

BLACKOUT

LUNCH #99–JOSE WONGS

CHUCK and CHARITY are being seated by waiter. Waiter is wearing simple white jacket (with Mexican motif embroidery?) and white pants.

CHARITY. (*as is being seated*) This is really a strange name for a Mexican restaurant. Jose Wongs?

CHUCK. Not really. In the Southwest this is quite a common type of name for a Mexican restaurant. You see, the immigration quotas for Mexicans were larger than those from China. So, many Chinese families moved to Mexico, intermarried and finally made the move to the United States. Very often these restaurants not only have good Mexican food, but also have great Chinese food.

CHARITY. Super. I'm in the mood for Chinese.

WAITER. Sorry, but if you'll look at the menu you'll only see Mexican food. The history lesson was quite revealing, but has no relevance to anything on the menu. So what do you want?

CHUCK. How about a new waiter?

(*During the following speeches the waiter is taken totally off guard. He has never been spoken to in such terms.*)

CHARITY. Chuck, we've handled waiters for . . . how many is it? . . . ninety-eight lunches. This guy doesn't stand a chance.

CHUCK. You're right. Listen, buster, you'd better take your best shot. There is nothing you can do or say to us that hasn't already been done or said. So, if you're trying to impress us with your arrogant attitude and insults, forget it! Now while we look at the menu, why don't you bring us two margaritas? (*WAITER Exits mumbling to himself.*)

CHARITY. But, Chuck, I've got to go back to the office. You know how hard it is for me to concentrate on business after I've had a drink or two.

CHUCK. Listen. I picked this place. I'm paying for it. In order to get the full cultural experience from this meal it must include these native drinks.

CHARITY. Are you sure that the margarita is a native Mexican drink and not something dreamed up by some American bartender?

CHUCK. Native! The Aztecs used to slam down a couple margaritas prior to sacrificing a virgin.

CHARITY. Sounds like a fraternity party.

WAITER. (*Enters with margaritas and chips and salsa.*) If you want these topless I can return them.

CHUCK. (*interest piqued*) *Topless?*

CHARITY. (*rising*) Now hold on, buster! I don't know what you've got in mind, but . . .

WAITER. Did you want them with no salt on the rim, topless or . . . salty, like your present dispositions?

CHUCK. Your humor is like pouring salt into a wound. So leave the drinks as they are and come back in a couple of minutes, and we'll have our order ready. Go annoy someone else with your colorful waiter sarcasm. You aren't dealing with a couple of rookies from out of town. Now, vamoose, muy pronto.

WAITER. That's it. Send the poor peon back into the field. (*continues to mumble as he Exits*)

CHUCK. Give us a break.

CHARITY. What got into you all of a sudden, Chuck? Have you secretly been taking assertiveness training classes?

CHUCK. I'm just fed up with all the waiters and their crummy manners and attitudes.

CHARITY. What happened to those wonderful characters to study?

CHUCK. I'd rather study foot fungus, thank you very much.

CHARITY. My, we are touchy today.

CHUCK. I'm sorry, Charity, but since this *is* our last lunch, I wanted it to be special.

CHARITY. It *is* special. I've never been to an authentic Mexican restaurant before.

CHUCK. That's not what I meant.

CHARITY. (*ignoring him*) What do you recommend? I don't know about anything on the menu except tacos and tostadas.

CHUCK. Charity, aren't you going to miss *our* lunches?

CHARITY. I'm going to miss all the bills. That waiter is going to be back soon, and we should be ready for him.

CHUCK. He can wait. That's what he's paid for . . . *waiting.* (*drinks*)

CHARITY. What's a chimichanga?

CHUCK. A chimichanga is meat, either chicken or beef, inside a deep-fried flour tortilla. It usually comes with sauce, sour cream and guacamole.

CHARITY. I think that's what I'll have. (*Eats a chip and salsa.*) Have you tried this sauce? It's really hot and spicy.

CHUCK. It's *salsa*, not sauce.

WAITER. (*Enters*) Are you ready to order . . . or did you plan on making a meal out of the chips?

CHUCK. (*stands*) Another smart aleck remark and they'll be making a *burrito* out of your *butt*! (*WAITER freezes then glances at own derriere.*)

CHARITY. Chuck, what's gotten into you? Now calm down, and let's give the nice gentleman our order. (*CHUCK sits.*) I'll have a chicken chimichanga. And, Chuck, what will you have?

CHUCK. I'll have the cheese enchiladas with rice.

WAITER. (*timidly*) Is that all? Do you need any more chips . . . or salsa . . . or possibly more of those salty margaritas?

CHARITY. No. We're fine. Thank you. (*WAITER Exits mumbling about "They think they're fine, they're not fine, etc.*) Chuck, I don't understand this behavior.

CHUCK. I'm just . . . concerned about your decision to have your play produced right away.

CHARITY. Why *write* one if you're not going to have the play *produced*? But, what could be wrong with it? I had the best teacher that any new playwright could have. Isn't it a good play?

CHUCK. Of course it is. It's just that. . . . are you sure an audience is ready for your *realistic* mystery, *Murder for Real*?

CHARITY. For years I've been attacking your characters that lack real depth.

CHUCK. Is that supposed to be news?

CHARITY. No. But this is my chance to prove that if the audience understands . . . really understands all the vital information that makes each character tick, it will add real motives to the murder mystery. It should also make them understand why exactly each murder takes place.

CHUCK. I still don't think the audience wants to know *too* much. You'll give them too much information to process.

CHARITY. You're just afraid you're wrong, and you don't want me to show you up.

CHUCK. Are you sure you can *take* the reviews as well as you can dish them *out*?

CHARITY. I'm ready to bare my chest to the world.

CHUCK. What? Charity, you'd better lay off the margaritas!

CHARITY. Literarily. I'm willing to open myself up to the slings and arrows of outrageous reviewers. (*Suddenly hit by the liquor. Giggles.*) I think you may be right. I'd better stop at *one* of these!

CHUCK. Charity, I'd like to talk about *us*.

CHARITY. *What* us?

CHUCK. You and me. I'm going to miss our lunches.

CHARITY. (*playfully*) You know you are the cheapest date I ever had. Too cheap to pay for your own lunches. You are *almost* a kept man. Letting an unsuspecting play reviewer pay for your keep.

CHUCK. Hey. We had a deal!

CHARITY. Big deal!

CHUCK. Will you listen to me for a moment? I've got some things I want to say.

CHARITY. Well, why don't you say them?

CHUCK. I'm trying to express my feelings . . . about . . .

CHARITY. Don't say anything else! Chuck, don't say anything that's going to ruin our last lunch. You're too serious. I just want to have a good time.

CHUCK. But, if I don't . . .

CHARITY. (*lifts glass*) Let's drink to *Murder for Real*.

CHUCK. But . . .

CHARITY. Don't be a party pooper, Chucky. Let's toast.

CHUCK. That's probably a good idea. We'd better toast it now, while we can. I don't think we're going to get another chance. (*lifts glass*) Here's to *Murder for Real*.

BLACKOUT.

(*LIVING ROOM: Daytime. No one onstage. Phone rings. GLINDA Enters from kitchen to answer it, and as she does so, CHUCK comes hurrying onstage in the middle of her on-phone lines.*

GLINDA. (*on phone*) Hello? . . . Yes, it is . . .

CHUCK. Is that for me—?

GLINDA. (*waves him silent, continues on phone*) I see . . . You've obviously called the wrong number . . . because everyone in this house has a functioning brain, and if we *wanted* to subscribe to your service, we'd know how to go about it without *your* help . . . (*listens a second, then hangs up phone, turns without explanation*) He hung up.

CHUCK. *Who* did?

GLINDA. Don't tell me you *want* old age health insurance?

CHUCK. Yesterday I would have said no. (*sits in chair*) Today I'm starting to feel I might need some.

GLINDA. Now, now, I'm *sure* she'll call!

CHUCK. I don't think so. And her *own* phone has been

disconnected, as of this morning. She must really hate me for coming on so strong. But I was so sure *she* felt the same way *I* did—

GLINDA. But why have her phone *disconnected*? She could just have the *number* changed.

CHUCK. I don't know. It doesn't make sense. I *thought* we were getting along just splendidly. After ninety-nine lunches together, I was *sure* we were. (*Doorbell; GLINDA starts that way but stops on:*) I'll get it. (*he opens door and CHARITY steps in, suitcase in hand*)

GLINDA. Why, Miss Starr! We were just *talking* about you!

CHUCK. Char, where have you *been*? I tried calling you, but . . .

CHARITY. I've given up my apartment. I didn't know where to turn, so while I'm regrouping my forces, at least—I was hoping you wouldn't mind if—if—I—

CHUCK. (*takes suitcase from her, instantly*) *Mind*?! Oh, honey, this is like a dream-come-true! Of *course* you can stay here! As long as you like! But—

GLINDA. —why did you give up your apartment?

CHARITY. (*almost in tears*) Had to. The rent's coming due, and it's not cheap, and I didn't want to blow most of my *severance*-pay on it!

CHUCK. What?! Oh, baby—! (*enfolds her into his arms—awkward with the suitcase, but he manages it, if clumsily*) You've lost your job?

CHARITY. They practically *snatched* it away! I've never been so hu-hu-humiliated in my life. (*sobs in his arms*) Called on the carpet, accused, condemned, and canceled, one-two-three!

GLINDA. Accused of *what*, Miss Starr?

CHARITY. Of going out to fancy lunches when I should have been reviewing plays!

GLINDA. Why didn't you *deny* it?

CHARITY. How could I? It was true!

CHUCK. But how could they *prove* such a thing?

CHARITY. They had *proof*! Restaurant names, dates, times—even what we had to eat!

GLINDA. (*the light dawns*) *Yolanda*! . . . Oh, this is terrible!

CHUCK. No! No, it's not! It's *perfect*!

CHARITY. (*pulls back from his embrace*) You're *happy* I got canned?!

CHUCK. Char, you don't *need* a job any more! I have a little surprise for you: Remember when you completed the first draft of your play?

CHARITY. Yes . . . ?

CHUCK. Well, I took a copy to Maury Jacobson.

CHARITY. Your *producer*?

CHUCK. And he *loved* it!

CHARITY. (*takes a horrified backstep from him*) But it wasn't even *polished* yet! I didn't have a chance to bolster the motivations, prune the deadwood out of the dialogue, pick up the pacing . . . ?!

CHUCK. Char, there's one rule I may not have mentioned during our ninety-nine lunches: Don't *ever* try to *improve* a script until you see it on its feet.

CHARITY. But there a *thousand* improvements I intended to make on that script, Chuck, and without them I don't see how the show can *possibly*—(*pauses; ponders; then:*) You say Maury *liked* it?

CHUCK. No. I said he *loved* it! Enough to start the production-wheels in motion!

GLINDA. Mister Reynolds! Do you mean he's going to produce it?

CHUCK. With the financial investment he's got in it already, he *has* to go ahead!

CHARITY. What financial investment?

CHUCK. He's contacted his backers, got the money, hired a cast, booked a rehearsal hall, picked a set-designer, mounted a publicity campaign—

CHARITY. *Wait*—wait—wait! This is all happening too fast for me to grasp. Why didn't you *tell* me?!

CHUCK. I was saving it for a surprise at our hundredth lunch.

CHARITY. And—just *when* do rehearsals *begin*?

CHUCK. Next Monday!

CHARITY. I think I'm going to be sick . . .

GLINDA. Spoken like a true playwright! Bathroom's down the hall.

CHUCK. Char, honey, you have *nothing* to be sick about!

CHARITY. (*starting down hallway*) Tell that to my stomach!

GLINDA. (*soothingly*) You're just not used to being unemployed!

CHUCK. (*correcting her*) *Self*-employed!

CHARITY. (*just short of Exit, turns and almost sobs:*) It's the same damn thing! (*then clasps hand over mouth and bolts out bathroomward during:*)

GLINDA. (*brightly*) But just think of all the money you're going to save on *lunches*! (*Offstage, we hear CHARITY make a sound somewhere between retching and screaming.*)

CHUCK. (*to GLINDA, amiably admonitory:*) You shouldn't have mentioned food.

The Curtain Falls

End of ACT TWO

ACT III

SCENE 1

LIVING ROOM: As the scene opens GLINDA is standing on chair working on CHUCK's tie.

GLINDA. As many of these opening nights as you've been to you'd think you'd learn how to tie these.

CHUCK. I just get so nervous my fingers don't want to cooperate with each other. The knot's too big. The end's too long. You always seem to tie it just right.

GLINDA. Do you want me to tie your shoes for you too?

CHUCK. Funny. But I've got news for you — no laces! (*points without looking*)

GLINDA. (*looks down then up*) Well, I've got news for you — no *shoes!*

CHUCK. (*looks at feet*) Where are my shoes?

GLINDA. Over by the chair where you set them.

CHUCK. (*Crosses to chair and sits to put on shoes.*) Normally, I'm cool and calm, but there's just something about opening night that makes me a basket case.

GLINDA. You think *you're* a basket case? Poor Charity hasn't been able to keep anything down for days. She has been frantic ever since you broke the news to her about her play already being in production. Frankly, the two of you are driving me *nuts.* This isn't even your show.

CHUCK. But it's the first play of Charity's, and since I taught her how to write, and used my influence to get Maury to produce it, I feel I have as much at stake as she does.

TERRY. (*Enters*) Dad, how soon are we going to leave?

CHUCK. In a few minutes. We're waiting on Charity.

79

TERRY. Has she stopped throwing up yet?

CHUCK. I hope so. Where's your tie?

TERRY. Only old fuddy-duddies wear ties. Besides ties cut off the circulation to your head and you could suffer brain damage. You wouldn't want *that*, would you? It could affect my grades.

CHUCK. Nonsense, *I've* worn ties for *years*, and it hasn't affected *me*! (*feels pockets*) Has anyone seen my wallet?

TERRY. I rest my case.

CHUCK. Okay. No tie. (*still trying to locate wallet*) But put on some real shoes. You can't wear tennis shoes with your slacks and jacket!

TERRY. You mean *leather* shoes?

CHUCK. What else?

TERRY. Dad, they don't let your feet breathe. You can develop some bad funguses. And your toes could rot off.

CHUCK. That's fungi. Leather breathes. Your toes are not going to fall off.

TERRY. Sorry, Dad, but I refuse to wear leather shoes.

CHUCK. Son, why are you giving me such a hard time? It would *really* make me happy if you wore leather shoes.

TERRY. Well, it wouldn't make *me* happy.

CHUCK. Terry!

TERRY. Dad, the reason wearing leather shoes would make me unhappy is that they're four sizes too small! You haven't bought me a pair in two years! You said why should you pay for a pair of shoes that I might wear only once or twice a year!

CHUCK. Why didn't you say so?!

TERRY. This way is more fun.

CHUCK. Driving your father to the brink of a nervous breakdown is fun?

TERRY. Why should you be so nervous? It's not *your*

opening. What is it that makes playwrights turn into basket cases on opening night? You practically have to have someone dress you, and Charity is constantly throwing up. I don't get it.

GLINDA. They're just sort of highstrung. It must be part of their creative make-up.

TERRY. You'd think they worked for the bomb squad.

CHUCK. Never say *bomb* on opening night!

TERRY. Is that some sort of theatrical superstition like not whistling backstage?

CHUCK. No. It's just a word we delete from our vocabulary until the reviews have come out.

TERRY. Don't we *want* this show to drop from the sky and explode!

CHUCK. Terry!

TERRY. Well, I didn't use the word. So what *do* we want? The guillotine method? Chop! The show's over! . . . Or a slow painful, tortuous run that lasts about four weeks before it's put out of its misery?

CHUCK. (*solemnly*) I want it to be successful.

TERRY. (*reacts*) Wait a minute, *I* thought that the idea was to give her the grief she's given *you*. You *want* her to get good reviews? I don't understand.

CHUCK. You don't need to understand. The first plan was to pay her back for her reviews. But, now I care too much for her to see her hurt.

TERRY. Darn!

CHUCK. Don't you like Charity?

TERRY. Yeah, but it's not going to be as much fun. I always enjoyed *Hamlet* more than *Romeo and Juliet*.

CHUCK. Sorry to disappoint you. Terry, have you seen my wallet?

TERRY. Yup.

CHUCK. Well, where is it?

TERRY. Right here. (*Reaches in pocket and pulls out wallet.*) You left it on the bathroom sink and I picked it up so you wouldn't have to go back after it.

CHUCK. Why didn't you tell me before?

TERRY. Because this way is . . .

CHUCK. More fun. (*CHARITY Enters, in evening gown, etc., turns to model her new attire.*) Char — you're totally gorgeous!

CHARITY. (*pauses, arms still extended from modeling, says mournfully:*) I hope I don't throw up in the car.

TERRY. (*sincerely*) I'm glad you're not sitting next to me.

GLINDA. I'm so excited! I *love* Broadway first-nights!

CHARITY. It's all happened so *fast*! (*sits on sofa*)

CHUCK. (*joins her on sofa, reassuringly*) It's theatre-economics. Maury can't *afford* to keep all those people on salary indefinitely with no money coming in.

CHARITY. But if only there'd been an out-of-town tryout first — !

CHUCK. *Nobody* goes out of town with a show any more. They can't take the expense, with the cost of producing Broadway shows these days. A few weeks of in-town previews is plenty.

GLINDA. (*to CHARITY:*) You really should have *gone* to the preview-shows, Miss Starr.

CHARITY. I got sick enough just watching *rehearsals*! (*to CHUCK:*) I *wish* you'd've come with me!

CHUCK. I couldn't. This is *your* baby! So I *helped* a little, sure, but once production was under way, I wanted *you* to have all the fun. Would you have *wanted* me there to suggest improvements?

CHARITY. (*after a pause*) No. No, I guess not. And it *was* exciting — even if I spent half my time in the ladies room.

TERRY. Hey, guys, we're going to be late!

CHUCK. (*stands*) You're right.

CHARITY. (*grabs CHUCK and pulls him back to sofa*) Oh, Chuck, do you think it'll play? I wish we weren't going to be sitting right beside Maury. He has such huge hands — and I have such a slender neck.

GLINDA. Producers never kill playwrights. Only themselves.

TERRY. I hope he does it with poison — I'd hate to get blood and brains on my new suit.

CHARITY. (*clutches stomach*) Terry!

TERRY. (*instantly contrite*) Sorry. I forgot about your stomach.

CHUCK. (*standing to leave*) Everybody got everything? (*ad-lib affirmatives from group*) Then let's go! (*All Exit except CHARITY who is rooted to sofa. After two beats, when they realize she's missing, all re-enter, spot her, and return to sofa.*)

CHARITY. Maybe I should wait here. You can all come back and *tell* me how it went.

CHUCK. (*sits on sofa next to CHARITY, taking her upper arm fondly.*) Char, you have *nothing*, to worry about! I've never seen a playwright with such meticulous devotion to detail — not even *myself*! You've covered *everything*. (*to TERRY and GLINDA:*) Do you know she even insisted on *actual* legal documents for the *prop* people?

GLINDA. But the audience won't be able to *see* what's on those papers?!

CHARITY. The *actors* will. I thought it would keep them in character.

CHUCK. More likely keep them in stitches.

CHARITY. So, I'm a nut for detail.

CHUCK. That's what Maury said — only he didn't use

words *that* kind. Your *detail* is costing him extra money.

CHARITY. Don't worry! It is detail like this that makes *Murder for Real* so different. If the actors feel that even the props are real, then the audience will feel that the play, with its realistic dialogue, is real. A totally new experience.

CHUCK. As long as you're convinced.

CHARITY. (*firmly*) I'm convinced! (*Stands, but grabs stomach.*) If I'm so convinced, why's my stomach doing flip-flops?

TERRY. Are we *going* to the play or are we going to *discuss* the play? If we're going to discuss the play, do I have time to get something to *eat*? There's a cold slice of sausage-and-pepperoni pizza in the refrigerator—

CHARITY. (*Suddenly puts hand over mouth and heads for bathroom.*) Excuse me. (*runs off*)

GLINDA. Can I help you? (*no response from CHARITY*) Poor kid. (*follows her*)

TERRY. (*CHUCK stares at TERRY; he avoids eye contact, but finally looks at his Dad.*) I'm sorry. I forgot. *Do* I have time?

CHUCK. For what?

TERRY. To get the pizza.

CHUCK. (*rises and approaches TERRY*) How can you think of *food* at a time like this? Besides, you just got *through* eating.

TERRY. (*shrugs*) Charity throws up. You forget things. I eat.

CHUCK. Well, it appears you're going to have plenty of .time! Just finish it before Charity comes back. (*TERRY Exits.*) Damn! I hate being late.

GLINDA. (*re-enters*) Just relax. Curtain is always a few minutes slow opening night.

CHUCK. But I won't have time to go to the *bar* before

curtain! (*starting to pace*) I like to have a glass or two of courage before the show starts. Tonight I might need three or four. Glinda, how are we going to get Charity to the *theater*? We can't even get her out of the *house*! And what about Maury? He's going to be upset if his playwright keeps going to the *restroom* all night! Maybe we should just stay here. (*sits on desk chair*)

GLINDA. You haven't missed an opening night yet, and you're not going to start tonight. I have taken the necessary precautions for Charity. (*Reaches in purse and pulls out handful of airline sickness bags.*) I also have a sandwich for Terry. (*Pulls out sandwich.*) And, for you . . . (*Pulls out miniature bottle of scotch.*) Always prepared. (*CHARITY re-enters.*)

CHARITY. I feel much better.

CHUCK. Good. Let's go. (*Grabs CHARITY by arm and starts heading for door.*)

GLINDA. Aren't you missing something?

CHUCK. (*stops, checking everything*) Got my wallet, (*looks down*) my shoes, (*reaches in pocket and pulls out keys*) my keys. All set! So lets go before something *else* happens! (*Exits with CHARITY; GLINDA remains; CHUCK re-enters.*) Well?

GLINDA. Shall we take *Terry* with us?

CHUCK. Aaaarrgh! Terry! Come on! We're going!

TERRY. (*Enters eating last bite of pizza.*) Coming.

CHUCK. Did you brush your teeth? Your breath smells like a garlic festival!

TERRY. Do you *want* me to brush my teeth? Or are we *going*?

CHUCK. Going! Just stay downwind of Charity.

TERRY. Dad, how can I stay downwind in the car?

GLINDA. Not to worry. (*Reaches in purse and pulls out breath spray.*) Let's go. (*TERRY takes spray and sprays mouth. They all start out door. Suddenly CHUCK returns with keys clenched in hand.)*

CHUCK. Where are my keys? (*GLINDA comes in, grabs his arm, bends it up so that his hand with keys are in front of face, puts his arm back in front of him and pushes CHUCK out door.)*

GLINDA. (*as exiting*) I'm sure glad I trained for this. Before I was a housekeeper I worked in a daycare center. Playwrights on opening night or precocious four year-olds, it's all the same.

LIGHTS DIM DOWN TO HALF. CLOCK HANDS SPIN TO SHOW ONE O'CLOCK. LIGHTS UP FULL ON SCENE TWO.

The moment the clock-hands indicate 1:00 a.m., the front door opens immediately, and our quartet re-enters, in a mood far removed from their off-to-the-theatre excitement when we last saw them a few seconds ago: TERRY carries his jacket over his arm, his shirttail half-untucked, GLINDA carries her dress shoes in one hand, CHUCK's bowtie now dangles from the breast pocket of his tux jacket, and CHARITY's up-swept-elegant in Scene One hairdo now hangs in helter-skelter coils all around her head, giving her a kind of hounddog-eared look. All four faces are more-or-less expressionless, bordering on grim and disgusted. They Enter in the foregoing order during this dialogue.

TERRY. *I* had to sit downwind of *her*!

GLINDA. I got the *window* rolled down in time, didn't I?

CHUCK. I wish I knew where to find an all-night car-wash! (*crosses to desk to hang tux coat on desk chair*)

CHARITY. I've never been so embarrassed and morti-
fied in my entire life!

TERRY. The *car* isn't going to take any medals for
pride, either!

GLINDA. I don't think she's referring to heaving her
guts onto the highway.

CHUCK. If she means her performance tonight at the
theatre, I don't want to discuss it.

CHARITY. You weren't *there* for it!

CHUCK. Ushers frown on men accompanying their
dates into the ladies room.

CHARITY. I'll never live tonight down, never!

GLINDA. Are you talking about the reaction of the
audience or the ladies room attendant?

CHARITY. Take your pick! I'll have to change my
name, move away, get into a new line of work —

TERRY. On the other hand, I didn't hear any of the
audience *complaining* about your show.

CHARITY. They were too busy *laughing* to complain.

CHUCK. Well, I *warned* you!

CHARITY. You what? (*slaps him on the shoulder*) You
never! You *encouraged* me to write that stupid play!

CHUCK. But not as a *realistic* murder-drama. I kept
telling you, people *laugh* at the truth!

CHARITY. What's so funny about cold-blooded
killing?!

TERRY. You gotta admit, when the first victim was
stabbed, his comment brought the house down!

GLINDA. (*musing*) What *was* it he said, exactly — ?

CHUCK. (*jumps at a chance to act*) Let me, let me!
(*dramatically mimics the actor's actions, glances under
hand clutching stomach "wound"*) Ouch! (*All except
CHARITY begin to laugh*)

CHARITY. That was *realism*! Daggers *hurt*! Think of
the horrible pain in his side!

GLINDA. The audience screamed louder than he did! (*All continue to laugh*)

CHUCK. Char, you're taking this much too hard.

CHARITY. I never want to see the inside of a theatre again as long as I live!

GLINDA. Really, Miss Starr, it's not as though you *saw* very much of the play.

TERRY. Good thing you weren't *reviewing* it. There's not much call for vivid descriptions of toilet bowls.

CHUCK. You must have seen *some* of it, Char!

GLINDA. No more than *I* did!

CHARITY. It was kind of you to accompany me to the lobby, Glinda.

GLINDA. That was protectionism. You had that suicidal look.

TERRY. How much of the show *did* you see?

CHARITY. The first four minutes.

CHUCK. Well, then, at least you caught the first twelve laughs.

CHARITY. I caught *all* of them!

GLINDA. Even in the *lobby*, we could *hear* the audience just fine.

CHARITY. The ladies room *door* couldn't keep the sound out!

GLINDA. It was like watching the little-girl figure on a Swiss clock; Charity would pop out the door, the audience would roar, she'd turn green and pop back in again.

CHUCK. (*cross to GLINDA*) Why didn't you go into the ladies room *with* her?

GLINDA. I've been to so many of *your* openings, the attendant's a personal friend of mine. I didn't want her to know I was chummy with the lady who was keeping her mop and bucket so busy.

(*DOORBELL rings.*)

TERRY. Are we expecting company?
CHARITY. It's probably the highway patrol with a cleaning bill!

(*DOORBELL rings again.*)

GLINDA. I'd better get that. Whoever it is, we deny *everything*! (*opens door and YOLANDA, with a topcoat over her nightgown and slippers, eagerly scurries in, rushes to CHUCK, takes his hands*)
YOLANDA. Chucky! I've been looking out the window and wondering! How did it go?
TERRY. Couldn't you see the side of the car?
YOLANDA. The what—?
GLINDA. Terry just means he wouldn't recommend you walk in our driveway *barefoot*!
TERRY. Yes I would.
CHARITY. Oh, *stop* it, *all* of you! This is not a *laughing* matter! I'm ruined!

(*As in a solemn litany:*)

TERRY. The car's ruined—
GLINDA. The highway's ruined—
CHUCK. The ladies room's ruined—
CHARITY. (*truly furious, now punctuates statements with foot stomping*) I said *stop* it! It's not funny! None of it is funny! *You're* not funny!
YOLANDA. (*at sea*) Who said anything was *funny*?
TERRY. Just the audience.
YOLANDA. But—I thought the play was a seriou murder-drama . . . ?!

CHARITY. Then you're the *only* one who thought so! (*bursts into tears and Exits to bedroom*)

YOLANDA. (*after a pause*) I take it—the opening didn't go well . . . ?

CHUCK. (*shrugs slightly*) *I* had a good time!

TERRY. Sure, you were *upwind*!

CHUCK. I mean at the theatre!

YOLANDA. (*half-embraces CHUCK and drags him to the sofa and pushes him onto it*) Well, whatever the reviewers say about the play, I know you did your very best. Miss Starr just doesn't *appreciate* your genius!

CHUCK. (*innocently*) I—I *did* try to warn her—

TERRY. Dad, you did *not*!

GLINDA. You kept telling her the play was *wonderful*!

CHUCK. It *was* wonderful! It still *is*! It may not be quite the play she *thought* it was, but—

(*All look as CHARITY re-enters, suitcase in hand.*)

CHARITY. (*with icy reserve*) Thank you all for your hospitality. I'll send for the rest of my things.

CHUCK. (*pulls free of YOLANDA*) Char, where are you going?

GLINDA. You'll never get a cab at this time of night!

TERRY. And your shoes will stick to the driveway!

CHARITY. (*has front door open*) It's a bit late for kind words I could have used earlier tonight! Goodbye. (*to CHUCK:*) It's been a real learning experience! (*Exits*)

CHUCK. (*Starts to go after her. Crosses to door.*) Char, what's gotten *into* you?!

TERRY. We already *know* what's come *out*!

YOLANDA. (*grabs CHUCK by the arm and swings him full circle back into the room*) Let her go! She's not worth it! Stay here, with me, where you belong!

CHUCK/GLINDA/TERRY. (*to YOLANDA:*) Oh, *shut up!*

CHUCK. (*pulls free, dashes out front door*) Charity, will you just *wait* a minute and *listen* to me . . . ? (*Then we hear him give a HOWL of surprise and chagrin, followed by the sound of a loud metallic crash; TERRY looks out front door, then turns to face the others for:*)

TERRY. I was wrong. He *didn't* stick to the driveway.

GLINDA. (*starts out the door*) Come on, help me get him out of the garbage can. (*Offstage, she will don a neck-to-floor robe and put a curler-cap over her hair to be dressed for* immediate *re-entry in Scene Three.*)

YOLANDA. (*still huffy after being unceremoniously shushed*) *Well!* I can see *I'm* not needed here!

TERRY. (*from just outside the door*) See? She's not as dumb as she looks!

(*All have exited, followed by a furious YOLANDA, who slams the door behind her; clock-hands twirl wildly to about 11:15 a.m., roomlight is replaced by cheery sunlight streaming through window.*)

SCENE 3

As scene opens, GLINDA, wearing robe, Enters from bedroom area, coffee cup in hand, and is surveying room for any cleaning that needs to take place. She begins the process of cleaning. CHUCK Enters from front door. He is wearing same clothes as before, although they look like he has slept in them. GLINDA gives him a long once-over.

GLINDA. You look terrible!

CHUCK. Everyone's a critic.

GLINDA. You look like something dragged out of *Terry's* room.

CHUCK. Impossible! Nothing comes out of his room alive. If it's edible it gets consumed. If it's not edible it's forever lost and is never heard from again.

GLINDA. You're lucky I don't have to clean his room. I'd ask for hazardous duty pay. Mister Reynolds, you look like you slept in those clothes.

CHUCK. (*crosses to sit on sofa*) In order to have slept in my clothes I'd have had to have slept.

GLINDA. Bad night? (*sits beside CHUCK*)

CHUCK. I couldn't sleep. I wasn't used to my *own* bed where I could stretch *out*. My body got *used* to sleeping in accordion-shape on the sofa. Every morning I'd get up and spend my first five minutes walking around like an ambulant question-mark.

GLINDA. Now that Charity's gone you can get *used* to your bed again. I never understood why you didn't just marry her and join her.

CHUCK. (*taken off guard*) What?

GLINDA. The bed's big enough for two.

CHUCK. (*stands and crosses left*) I am surprised at you, Mrs. Bellows! Charity and I are . . . were . . . just good friends. I merely was helping her out. After all, it sorta was my fault that she got fired. I felt a responsibility to her. Our relationship was just platonic. Romance never entered my thoughts.

GLINDA. Are you kidding?! You took more cold showers than an entire Eskimo village.

CHUCK. What about Terry? I don't think a marriage of convenience is the kind of example a father should set.

GLINDA. Come on! He's seen *Dynasty*.

CHUCK. Well, it's too late now. (*crosses to chair*) She's gone.

GLINDA. You miss her already, don't you?

CHUCK. I think that's why I couldn't sleep. I should have taken the playwriting lessons seriously. Instead of doing her job, she was having lunch with me. She loses her job and gets totally embarrassed when her play that I taught her to write turns out be one big joke. So, when I couldn't sleep I decided to go for a walk, trying to sort things out.

GLINDA. Did you come to any conclusions?

CHUCK. Yeah. It's not *safe* out there! There are some real strange and weird people just outside the door. I only planned on walking few minutes. But, in my attempt to avoid or lose some desperate-looking characters, it took me several hours just to get back here. I forgot how dangerous it is out there after dark.

GLINDA. But what about Charity?

CHUCK. Oh, *she* wouldn't have been any help.

GLINDA. (*trying to get CHUCK back on track*) No, no. What are you going to *do*?

CHUCK. I'm going to get better locks for the door!

GLINDA. (*firmly; standing and cross to CHUCK*) Listen, *Chuckles*, you're never going to forgive yourself if you let her go without even trying to get her back. Now are you going to try to get her back or are you going to run around like some whipped dog, with your tail tucked between your legs?

CHUCK. I wouldn't know where to start. I don't know where she's staying. She doesn't have a job to contact her at. Why did I let her go? (*Suddenly TERRY Enters front door with arms full of newspapers, which he deposits on sofa. His mood is cheery and positive.*) Where have you been?

TERRY. (*happily*) I've been out stealing newspapers again.

CHUCK. Terry! I thought we'd broken you of that habit. You ought to be ashamed of yourself. Instead, you looked pleased with yourself.

TERRY. I didn't want the neighbors to read Charity's reviews. So . . .

CHUCK. You figured that if you stole the papers, they *couldn't* read them?

TERRY. Right. But . . .

CHUCK. You're sorry you did, because . . .

TERRY. It was unnecessary.

CHUCK. Terry, theft is never necessary.

TERRY. Yeah, especially when the reviews are great.

CHUCK. Right! Especially when. . . . Did you say the reviews are great?

TERRY. I read the reviews, and they're *terrific*! The critics loved it! One even said that one of their own had become a comic genius.

CHUCK. Let me see those. (*TERRY hands him some of the papers. CHUCK begins reading the reviews.*)

GLINDA. Terry, by the way, why aren't you in school?

TERRY. (*with big smile*) *Bus drivers'* strike. School's cancelled. That's why the papers were still out. Mothers and kids are sleeping *in* this morning.

CHUCK. (*reading from reviews*) "*Murder for Real* is campy fun. . . . Audience slaughtered from laughter. . . . Is there a chiropractor in the audience? Opening night audience falling out of chairs, literally, from laughing so hard. . . . Characters so "real" that they are perfectly satirical. . . . Has created a new standard for comedy mystery. . . . Is a real hoot! The comedy hit of the century." (*looks up from reviews*) I would *kill* for reviews like these. (*There is a knock at the door.*

GLINDA crosses and opens the door. CHARITY Enters.)

CHARITY. I . . . uh . . . packed all my dresses but none of my underwear.

CHUCK. I was just reading your review. Have you seen it?

CHARITY. Uh . . . yes . . . I have. I figure I should leave town before I'm laughed out of town. I should have listened to you. You tried to warn me about my realistic characters. I tried to write the ultimate realistic murder mystery play, and everyone thinks that it was the funniest thing they've ever seen. Do you have a paper bag I could wear to the bus depot?

CHUCK. I'm so glad you came back.

CHARITY. Me too. My mother always wanted me to wear clean underwear wherever I went. (*moves to sofa and starts to cry.*) Chuck, how can I ever show my face around New York again? I thought I could write a good *serious* play.

CHUCK. (*goes to her*) Char, sweetheart, don't you realize the talent you have? You have the talent to write comedy. You have the ability to make people laugh.

CHARITY. But I was trying to write *truth*!

CHUCK. Don't you realize that *all* comedy is based on the truth? It's the hardest type of stage-writing there is. Thousands would *die* for the ability to write what *you* wrote and to get the reviews that *you* just got.

CHARITY. But, I feel so foolish! And, I . . .

CHUCK. Not another word. (*Tries to kiss CHARITY.*)

CHARITY. (*breaks away, stands moves* D.R.) You're just trying to make me feel better. Your first playwriting student totally embarrasses you.

CHARITY. (*follows CHARITY* D.R.) You've made me proud. The woman I care about turns out to be the best comedy playwright of the decade.

CHARITY. Chuck, we've had fun during the lunches. You're a very good playwright. You taught me a great deal about playwriting. So you think the student has fallen in love with the teacher?

CHUCK. I care about you.

CHARITY. (*very businesslike*) You are a very nice person to take me under your wing to teach me playwriting and to take me into your home when I needed a place to stay.

CHUCK. Charity, I love you. (*grabs her*)

CHARITY. (*still businesslike*) Chuck, as much as I admire you both as a person and a creative artist, I don't think your continuing insistence on a more *romantic* relationship is founded in reality. (*CHUCK abruptly grabs her in his arms and kisses her, firmly; she does not embrace him, but does not struggle, either.*)

(*The following is like watching a tennis match. CHUCK and CHARITY on* D.R. *and TERRY and GLINDA by desk.*)

TERRY. (*during kiss*) Should I close my eyes?

GLINDA. No. This is a *learning* experience.

CHARITY. (*when CHUCK pulls back for air*) *Really*, now, Chuck, do you actually believe that sheer physical force can—(*he kisses her again, even better*)

TERRY. I thought Charity *liked* Dad?

GLINDA. She's *bananas* about him!

CHARITY. (*when he disengages*)—have any effect on my perfectly reasonable attitude that just because two people—(*he kisses her again,* very *much better*)

TERRY. She doesn't *act* bananas about him!

GLINDA. It's too soon for that.

CHARITY. (*when kiss ends*) Chuck, you're wasting

your time. Yes, I like you, but—(*stupendous kiss; this time her arms go slightly about his neck, but then withdraw the moment he pauses for breath*)

TERRY. What do you mean"too soon"?

GLINDA. The moment she *admits* she likes him, he'll stop *kissing* her!

CHARITY. (*kiss breaks*) Chuck, this is ridiculous! What will people think if you continue to—(*fantastic kiss, in which she hungrily joins, embrace and all*)

TERRY. I *think* I understand her point of view—but she's got to tell him the truth *sometime*!

GLINDA. Sure, but then he'll want to *talk* about it!

CHARITY. (*breaks away again as he breaks for air*) Now, look, my—my mind is made up, and—(*he kisses her again–she helps*)

TERRY. Doesn't *she* want to talk about it?

GLINDA. It's a toss-up: talking or kissing. Which would *you* pick?

CHARITY. (*break for air*) Mere *physical* contact has no relation to mature—(*once more, with feeling from them both*)

TERRY. I think she's starting to kiss him back a little harder!

GLINDA. That's so he'll think he's making progress.

CHARITY. (*breath*) Chuck, I . . . (*here we go again!*)

TERRY. I think he's just about kissed out.

GLINDA. That's why she's helping him.

TERRY. Shouldn't we get into the act about now?

GLINDA. For all the good it'll do us. Watch–! (*to CHUCK:*) Sir, can't you see you're wasting your time?

CHARITY. (*breaks current kiss long enough to announce:*) Butt out! (*back to kiss*)

GLINDA. See what I mean?

CHARITY. (*finally pushes CHUCK away backwards–*

he ends up sitting on coffee table) Chuck, this is ridiculous—

CHUCK. Okay, I give up, you *don't* give a damn about me!

GLINDA. Nonsense. This woman has been crazy about you from the moment she set eyes on you!

CHARITY. Now really, Glinda—!

GLINDA. I can *prove* it! (*steps to desk and takes out scrapbook*) Here, Mister Reynolds, take a look at her review of HOW TO MURDER A MILLIONAIRE!

CHUCK. Listen, Glinda, this morning is going badly enough without re-opening old wounds!

TERRY. How did that review get into the scrapbook?

GLINDA. Your father saves *all* reviews, Terry, good *or* bad. He loves to see his name in print.

CHUCK. (*crosses to GLINDA*) I don't remember pasting *that* one into the book!

GLINDA. Why should you? You always end up leaving the clippings for *me* to catalogue, remember?

TERRY. But I thought that review was all chopped up, when you pretended you were cutting shopping coupons out of the paper?

CHARITY. Shopping coupons?

TERRY. It's a long story.

CHUCK. (*who has been, reluctantly, trying to find the spot in the scrapbook, finds it*) Here it is . . . Wait a minute! What's this caption over the review—"A *SECOND* LOOK AT 'HOW TO MURDER A MILLIONAIRE'"—?!

GLINDA. This is from the *Late Morning* edition, the edition Charity brought along *with* her when she first entered this house the day after your show opened with a big apologetic red ribbon on it!

CHUCK. (*reading, his eyes widening, getting incredu-*

lous, just mumbling bits and pieces) "A truly *brilliant* mystery . . . mind-boggling revelations . . . delightful characters . . . one surprise after another . . . the best play of this season . . ." (*lowers paper, stares at CHARITY, stunned*) This is the best review I ever got in my *career*! I don't get it. What's going on here?!

CHARITY. (*squirming with embarrassment*) Well . . . you see . . . after that *first* edition came out . . . when every other newspaper in town came out with an absolute *rave* about your show . . .

GLINDA. Your editor called you on the carpet and said "What the hell"?

CHARITY. And that's putting it *mildly*!

TERRY. (*catches on*) So you wrote this *great* review to save your job!

CHUCK. I *still* don't get it! I mean, I understand what you all just said, but—Charity, why didn't you *tell* me, that morning, when you first showed up here?

CHARITY. Well—I—I—you see—

GLINDA. Let *me* carry the ball!

CHARITY. Yes. Please.

GLINDA. (*to CHUCK:*) The moment she set eyes on you, she fell head-over-heels, that's what happened.

TERRY. So she didn't want to just turn over the new review, apologize for the first review—

CHARITY. Which my editor *insisted* I do . . .

GLINDA. And then walk out of your life forever!

CHUCK. Charity—is this true? You *made up* all that stuff about coming to me for playwriting consultation?

TERRY. Well, *sure* she did. She *told* us that, the first day she was here!

CHUCK. And you never told *me* . . . ? Why not?!

TERRY. Well, for one thing, Charity's got great legs!

CHUCK. (*turns to CHARITY*) In other words, you've

lied to me about your feelings for months and months — because you really *are* in love with me?!

CHARITY. From the moment I set eyes on you!

CHUCK. You're despicable!

CHARITY. (*slowly starts to move toward CHUCK, nodding sadly*) Totally.

CHUCK. Untrustworthy!

CHARITY. (*getting closer*) Absolutely!

CHUCK. A sexpot in sheep's clothing!

CHARITY. (*reaching arms-length-face-to-face*) I'm afraid so.

CHUCK. I hope you're prepared to pay the penalty. (*TERRY now watching closely from behind & between them.*)

CHARITY. (*sighs*) Ready as I'll ever be.

CHUCK. Good. (*grabs her, kisses her*) Take that! (*kisses again*) And that! (*kisses again*) And that! And (*does a magnificent kiss, in which she happily assists; after a bit:*) that!

TERRY. (*to GLINDA, indignantly:*) *Look* at them!! When *I* tell lies, I get sent to bed without my supper!

CHARITY. (*shrugs*) What's *food*?! (*She and CHUCK kiss again, rapturously.*)

GLINDA. Food is what we're going to have in just a few minutes. Since it's too late to have breakfast I hope you don't mind an early lunch.

TERRY. Great! I'm starved.

GLINDA. I figured that this would be a special morning, so I planned a special lunch. Everyone take a seat. (*TERRY, CHUCK, and CHARITY take seats. CHUCK and CHARITY sit as close as they can to each other. Romance is in their eyes.*) Everyone pardon me just a moment. (*She Exits into the kitchen.*)

CHARITY. How did she know this was going to be a

special morning? Isn't it kind of early for lunch?

CHUCK. Sweetheart, this is our *one hundredth* lunch. And I think that this is a wonderful time to be having it. (*They kiss.*)

TERRY. Glinda, they're doing it again! Will you two cut it out? I'm trying to keep my appetite.

CHUCK. How would you like to have your lunch in your room?

GLINDA. (*Enters. Places silverware, plates and wine glasses. Then yells to kitchen.*) Any time! (*Takes seat.*)

(*WAITER Enters with covered serving dishes of food which he sets on table.*)

CHUCK. What is going on here? (*WAITER starts pouring champagne. Pulls out bottle of pop from champagne bucket when he reaches TERRY.*)

GLINDA. Since this was such a special occasion I decided to have this lunch *catered.* I didn't want to miss out on the fun.

CHUCK. (*Takes a good look at the WAITER.*) Wait a minute! Aren't you . . .

CHARITY. (*looks at WAITER*) We've seen you before.

WAITER. (*as pouring*) I can't believe it! I left the restaurant business so I could *avoid* you two! I was afraid you'd come back. You two have left a path of waiters in your wake. I'm sure the analysts have been doing a great business.

GLINDA. I gather you folks *know* each other?

WAITER. (*as laying out plates*) I only encountered them once but their reputation swept through the waiter community causing fear to all those who heard. It was like a plague, wiping out poor innocent waiters. They were afraid to go to work. Even members of my family quit what had been a truly noble family profession. A few of us started our own catering company. But some poor souls couldn't face food anymore and have become mechanics. Yuck! (*almost pleading*) Please be gentle.

CHUCK. You're breaking my heart. (*to CHARITY:*) Shall we let this poor knave off the hook?

CHARITY. Chuck, honey, since this is our one hundredth lunch, it would be nice to have some atmosphere to remind us of the other ninety-nine. Don't you sort of miss the arrogant wisecracks and clever waiter patter?

CHUCK. Whatever you say. (*to WAITER:*) Give us your best snooty waiter routine. You can practice up in case the catering business doesn't work out.

WAITER. Are you sure? It would be fun.

CHUCK. Lay on, MacDuff!

TERRY. Are you sure I'm old enough for this?

GLINDA. Consider this preparation for latter life — an important educational experience.

WAITER. Oh this is going to be such a fun luncheon. I'll have to wake all the winos and let them know about it on my way home. Of course, if a cab driver starts getting rude I can always make him suffer through an in-depth description of this happy event. That'll teach 'em!

CHARITY. Doesn't this bring back memories?

CHUCK. It is wonderful. (*They embrace and kiss.*)

TERRY. Is this appropriate mealtime behavior?

GLINDA. After all they've gone through, they've earned it.

WAITER. Oh goodie! I won't have to provide entertainment. We can just watch these two kids at the malt shop. I get it — you're practicing mouth to mouth resuscitation. If you two don't mind, we'd like to keep our food down, if you know what I mean.

GLINDA. (*lifts glass*) Here's to *Murder for Real* and the best new comedy playwright of the decade.

CHUCK. (*lifts glass*) Here's to one hundred lunches and to the woman with whom I plan on spending one hundred thousand more.

CHARITY. (*lifts glass*) Here's to the best mystery playwright, the best comedy playwright teacher and the man I love!

TERRY. (*lifts glass of pop*) Here's to the bus drivers!

(*CHUCK and CHARITY kiss and hold it until curtain.*)

END OF ACT THREE

CURTAIN

Production Notes

The waiters *should be played by the same actor.* This makes the role a real delight for the actor and the audience — and fits into idea that the waiters are all related. Each waiter should have its own distinct personality. The waiter in Act 3 may be any of the waiters — however, it should be one of the snooty waiters.

The change from restaurant to Chuck's home and vice versa could be done several ways. The original show was done with a one-half revolve and the changing of panels behind Chuck and Charity, as well as changing menus, table cloths, etc. It could be done effectively with isolation using light or just by changing table cloths, napkins, etc.

Costume changes in Act 2 are tricky, but can be done within the interlude times. Some of it can be helped by layering and using different combinations of several different outfits. However, in the original show Charity and the waiters each had totally different outfits for each restaurant and was ready in plenty of time.

Props

Act 1

Pair of shoes-one with small cup to hold water
Tuxedo and tie scattered about room
Watch, Glinda
Bunch of newspapers
Manhattan Journal with holes from coupon removal
Cut-out review
Coffee server, cups on tray
Sack lunch

School books and notebook
Paper with bow brought by Charity
Adhesive tape
Large knife
Book on plotting by George Polti

Act 2

Chateau Jasper

Table and two chairs
2 place settings
2 napkins
Table cloth
2 menus
2 iced teas
Comic book
Jumbo shrimp cocktail

Interlude

dust rag
apple (or sandwich)

Hymie's

Stained table cloth
Stained menu
Serving tray
2 bowls of hash
2 forks
Prop money

Interlude

Apple
TV remote control

Four Seasons

Table cloth
2 place settings
2 napkins
2 menus
2 glasses water
Bottle champagne

Interlude

Comic book
Novel

Kali's

Table cloth
2 place settings
2 napkins
2 menus
Prop pistol for o.s. shots
Prop money in Charity's purse

Wally's

Ketchup, mustard, relish, and onion containers
Folder with plot outline, character descriptions, etc.
Knife carried by Evelyn
2 beers
2 hot dogs
2 buns
Menu on wall

Interlude

School books
Purse

Pierre's

Table cloth
2 place settings
2 glasses water
2 napkins
Cordial glass with Benedictine
Cordial glass with Courvoisier
Folder with bill

Interlude

TV remote control

Jose Wong's

Table cloth
2 glasses water
2 place settings
2 menus
Bowl of tortilla chips
Bowl of salsa
2 margaritas in salted glasses

Interlude

Suitcase

Act Three

Wallet in Terry's pocket
In Glinda's purse: airsick bag, sandwich, miniature
    scotch bottle, breath spray
Keys
Suitcase
Newspapers
Scrapbook
4 wine glasses
Bottle of champagne
Bottle of pop

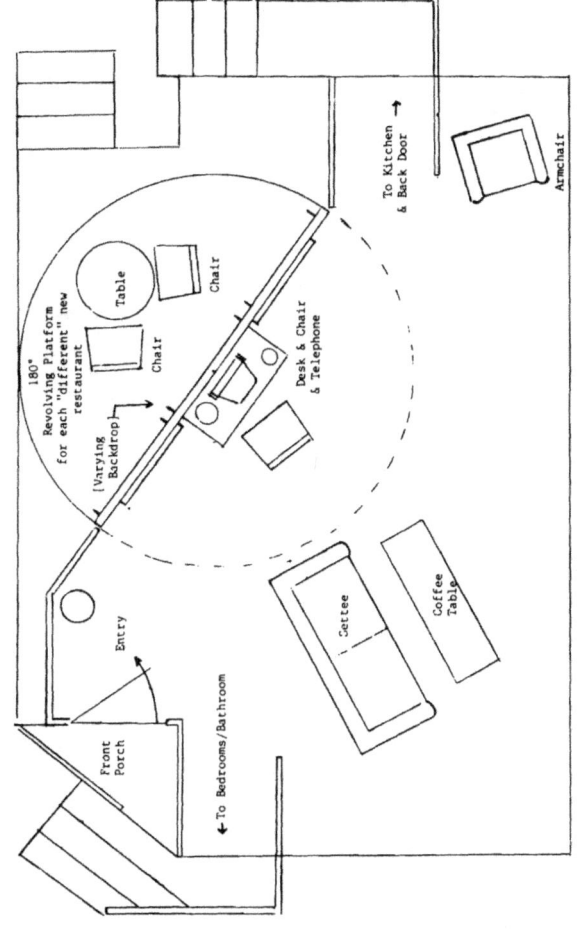

"100 LUNCHES"

- Stage Setting -

Armchair

To Kitchen & Back Door

Chair

Table

Chair

180° Revolving Platform for each "different" new restaurant

Desk & Chair & Telephone

Varying Backdrop

Settee

Coffee Table

Entry

Front Porch

To Bedrooms/Bathroom

109

www.ingramcontent.com/pod-product-compliance
Lightning Source LLC
Chambersburg PA
CBHW070334120726
47909CB00008B/2694